Kiet and the Golden Peacock

Other Superintendent Bamsan Kiet novels
by Gary Alexander

PIGEON BLOOD
UNFUNNY MONEY

Kiet and the Golden Peacock

Gary Alexander

ST. MARTIN'S PRESS

NEW YORK

The author apologizes to the Socialist Republic of the Union of Burma, the People's Republic of China, the Laotian People's Democratic Republic, and the Kingdom of Thailand for geographic distortions and for encroachment on their borders. Tolerance is also asked for liberties taken with the topography and climate of the region.

DESIGN BY BARBARA M. BACHMAN

Library of Congress Cataloging-in-Publication Data

Alexander, Gary.
    Kiet and the golden peacock : a Superintendent Bamsan Kiet mystery
/ Gary Alexander.
       p.   cm.
    "A Thomas Dunne book."
    ISBN 0-312-03372-9
    I. Title.
PS3551.L3554K54   1989
813'.54—dc20   89-34835
                                                                            CIP

First Edition

10 9 8 7 6 5 4 3 2 1

FOR
NADINE AND ROY DUENSING

Cast of Characters
with Pronouncing Guide
for Asian Names

Bamsan Kiet (bomb-sawn key-yet), Hickorn's superintendent of police

Captain Binh (bin), Kiet's adjutant

Prince Novisad Pakse (nove-ih-said pock-see), ruler of Luong

Gaston LaCroix, manager of the Hickorn Continental Hotel

Ambassador Smithson, U.S. ambassador

Fop Tia (full'p tee-ah), former mayor of Hickorn

Phorn Ridsa (forn rid-suh), minister of tourism

Ambassador Dang, Vietnamese ambassador

Lin Aidit (lin i'd-it), tour guide

Charles "Chick" Chipperfield, American entrepreneur

Alvin "Ambulance Al" Selkirk, American entrepreneur

Dr. Latisa Chi (lat-ih-saw chee), curator of the National Museum

Quoc (kwock), leprous beggar with no nose

Mai Le Trung (my-lee-trung), Vietnamese embassy cultural attaché

Tui Nha (too-ey nah), rice broker

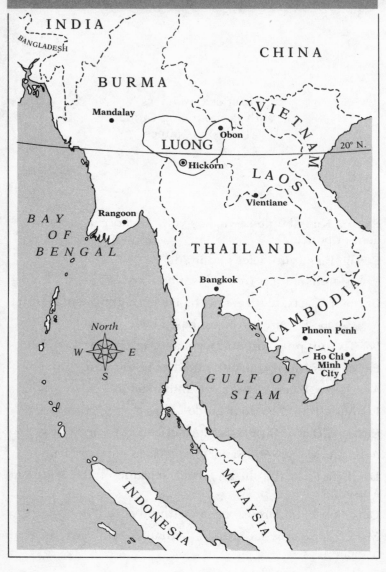

The Kingdom of
LUONG

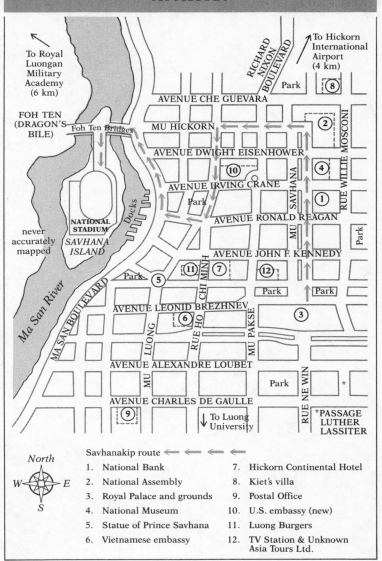

Downtown
HICKORN

To Royal
Luongan
Military
Academy
(6 km)

To Hickorn
International
Airport
(4 km)

RICHARD NIXON BOULEVARD

FOH TEN
(DRAGON'S
BILE)

Foh Ten Bridges

Park

AVENUE CHE GUEVARA

MU HICKORN

AVENUE DWIGHT EISENHOWER

AVENUE IRVING CRANE

Park

AVENUE RONALD REAGAN

MU SAVHANA

RUE WILLIE MOSCONI

Docks

NATIONAL
STADIUM

never
accurately
mapped

SAVHANA
ISLAND

AVENUE JOHN F. KENNEDY

Ma San River

MA SAN BOULEVARD

Park

RUE HO CHI MINH

AVENUE LEONID BREZHNEV

MU LUONG

RUE HO CHI MINH

MU PAKSE

Park

Park

AVENUE ALEXANDRE LOUBET

MU

Park

RUE NE WIN

AVENUE CHARLES DE GAULLE

To Luong
University

*PASSAGE
LUTHER
LASSITER

North

W — E

S

Savhanakip route ⟸ ⟸ ⟸ ⟸

1. National Bank
2. National Assembly
3. Royal Palace and grounds
4. National Museum
5. Statue of Prince Savhana
6. Vietnamese embassy

7. Hickorn Continental Hotel
8. Kiet's villa
9. Postal Office
10. U.S. embassy (new)
11. Luong Burgers
12. TV Station & Unknown
    Asia Tours Ltd.

The essence of the gentleman is that of wind;
the essence of small people is that of grass.
And when a wind passes over the grass, it
cannot choose but bend.

—CONFUCIUS

Prologue

The Kingdom of Luong is a fancy, a figment.

It is not a Southeast Asian backwater surrounded by China, Burma, Laos, and Thailand.

It is not a former French colony that was granted independence in 1954.

It is not sometimes known as the Fourth Indochina.

It is not a country that was spared a war of national liberation because of its ability to feed itself and a pervasive political apathy.

Nor is its largest city, the capital of Hickorn, a sleepy metropolis of 220,000 located in the lush of lowlands on the Ma San River.

Nor is it a constitutional monarchy ruled by seventy-eight-year-old Prince Novisad Pakse, a man whose abiding passion is pocket billiards.

Nor does Prince Pakse straddle a neutralist fence by the simple act of naming and renaming Hickorn's streets in honor of powerful foreigners.

Nor is Luong attempting of late to attract hard currency

1

through the promotion of tourism (the Luongan zin being virtually unknown, let alone traded, on international money markets).

Nor is Hickorn Superintendent of Police Bamsan Kiet dreading his first taste of American fast food.

But *if* the above were true . . .

1

"One hundred percent beef," Captain Binh was explaining. "Flash frozen and shipped by air from an Iowa packing house. Quality and freshness are ensured."

Hickorn Superintendent of Police Bamsan Kiet lifted the bun of his Luong Burgers cheeseburger deluxe. Tendrils of a melted substance identified as American cheese clung to it and the perfectly circular meat patty inside. "Splendid," he said. "No doubt very wholesome."

"And delicious," Binh said, biting into his second cheeseburger deluxe. He chewed, gulped happily, and said, "Superintendent, have I told you how much I miss cheeseburgers?"

"Occasionally," Kiet said, nibbling at his.

Captain Binh, Kiet's young adjutant, had trained for a year with the police department of the United States federal capital, the District of Columbia. He had brought home extraordinary tales of SWAT teams, computerized administration, drug raids, and court backlogs. Binh had also acquired a liking for certain aspects of Western culture, fast food and television among them. Today, Kiet had finally yielded and agreed to try the first. He knew that he would soon give in and sample the joys of the second.

Kiet chewed cautiously and watched Binh devour his lunch. Where did it all go? Binh in his starched white uniform with gold captain's pips gleaming on shoulder boards was thin and wiry. The greases and sugars would slide through him.

Kiet was a contrast—middle-aged, given to midsection bulk, attired casually in slacks, white shirt, and sandals. He swallowed, contemplating the injustice of flavorless calories straining his waistline even further.

He could see through the windows of Luong Burgers across Rue Ho Chi Minh to the *terrasse* of the Hickorn Continental Hotel. The Continental's luncheon specialty was shrimp netted from the Ma San River, fried in peanut oil, and garnished with sauces and chopped peppers. Wash those glorious freshwater shellfish down with iced bottles of Golden Tiger beer and the gastronomical indiscretion was well worth the price.

But here he was, sitting on a molded plastic bench in a large room decorated with posters of Asian cities, listening to Luongan folk tunes wafting from hidden speakers, in the company of American and Japanese tourists. The visitors wore Hawaiian shirts and ate hungrily, Nikons and Minoltas strapped around their necks.

Kiet was paying another price, the price of continued harmony with his second-in-command. Binh gobbled a cluster of French fries. Kiet took one from his foam carton. It was crunchy, the texture of a crustacean leg, but any taste had been obliterated by oily crystals of salt. Binh drank from his milkshake cup. The flavor of the day was rare tropical fruit. Kiet did the same and was reminded of chemistry.

"Well?" Binh asked eagerly.

"Palatable."

"You're not really getting into your burger, Superintendent. It'll get cold."

"Well," Kiet said. He picked up and studied the individual packages of catsup, mustard, mayonnaise, and pickle relish that had been provided with his purchase. He put them down and poured nic sau onto his perfectly circular meat patty. Nic sau was a fish sauce, a condiment used as universally by Luongans as catsup by Americans. He then spooned on sliced peppers, a fiery variety even by Luongan standards.

"Better," Kiet said, his mouth full.

"Superintendent, you're compromising the authenticity of your meal!"

"What authenticity? Luong had no burgers until we imported them from the American province of Iowa. That is an extreme compromise. The only things Luongan about this sandwich are the peppers and nic sau I added."

"Western travelers are finicky," Binh said. "Some won't eat spicy foods, and the familiarity of an establishment such as Luong Burgers is comforting."

Kiet resisted telling Binh that it should therefore be called what it really is. Tear down the *Luong* in the Luong Burgers sign. Remove the posters. Replace the folk music with skull-throbbing rock and roll.

He kept silent more out of preoccupation than concern for Binh's feelings. Savhanakip, Luong's annual celebration, was less than a week away and many security details had not been completed. Informal revelry had already begun, mostly in the form of public drunkenness. From a law enforcement standpoint, Savhanakip was a headache, not a festival.

Binh swiveled in his chair and looked outside.

"I can see the sidewalk, Captain. I will inform you if he returns."

Kiet was referring to a leprous beggar who had been pestering Luong Burgers customers. The café manager had complained to Hickorn Police Headquarters. Binh volunteered to answer the complaint personally and persuaded Kiet to accompany him. "We can serve the public and savor a treat at the same time," he said. A "two-fer," he termed it.

"I don't suppose you've tried out your TV yet," Binh said. "If you had, I suppose you'd've told me."

"Soon," Kiet said as he doused his French fries with nic sau. Two American businessmen of dubious character who had collaborated with Luongan officials to create Unknown Asia Tours Ltd. were also the owners of Luong Burgers. As a sop to the Ministry of Tourism, they had installed Hickorn's—and Luong's—first television station. It had been in operation for a month.

Authorizations and permits for the Unknown Asia Tours enterprise had raced through Luong's sluggish bureaucracy in a sprint, a reward attributed to this generosity. The suspicious Kiet doubted that a television transmitting facility was the only gratuity lubricating the process.

Binh smiled. "I'll bet it isn't even out of the box."

Unknown Asia Tours Ltd. had given television receivers to Hickorn's most prominent businessmen and municipal leaders, Kiet included. His was, indeed, still in its colorful wrapping on his kitchen table. His cat was using it as a pedestal bed.

"Soon," Kiet said, munching. The potatoes were suddenly delicious.

"Every room in the Continental has one now, you know. They're equipped with coin slots."

"Practical. Further familiarity for tourists in search of exotic Asia." The advertised purpose of Unknown Asia Tours was to open an off-the-beaten-track window for those adventurous souls willing to risk the unusual. Luong was sandwiched into an itinerary that included Indonesia, Burma, and Sri Lanka. Kiet's experience with the travelers had led him to conclude that the majority were either

6

academic types or budgeters who could not afford the crazed prices of Tokyo and Hong Kong.

Binh's smile became a laugh. "Don't be so cynical, Superintendent. You're fortunate to have a free television. You should give it a chance. I'm going to buy one the instant I've saved enough money. They are awfully expensive, despite being black-and-white. The transmitter is old and secondhand. Oh, how you would love viewing color on a large screen!"

Kiet nodded, conceding Binh's point on the cost. The tiniest receivers were being sold in chic Hickorn shops for the equivalent of two hundred American dollars, nearly half the average Luongan's annual income. Signs of financial sacrifice were appearing on Hickorn's skyline— sticklike aluminum aerials that plucked signals from the air.

He said, "Hickorn has two radio stations and a dozen cinemas. Television is superfluous."

"TV is the best of both worlds, Superintendent. The sounds of radio plus theater video. In your very own home. At the twist of a knob."

"I am told that the television programs donated with the transmitting apparatus—"

"Packaged," Binh interrupted. "Packaged with the station. A package deal, free, gratis."

Kiet answered with a sigh. Thankfully, Luong Burgers' air conditioning system was still on order, not yet assaulting him like an arctic storm. The ninety-degree, ninety-percent-humidity atmosphere was quite pleasant. He sipped his rare tropical fruit milkshake. It bothered him slightly that the milkshake's alleged ice cream base had not melted, that it remained congealed.

"They didn't have to provide those shows, Superintendent."

"Yes, but the package programs are likewise old and secondhand, are they not?"

7

"I've watched the shows in stores displaying TVs, Superintendent," Binh said, wide-eyed. "They're wonderful series episodes from the 1950s and 1960s. Westerns."

Kiet nodded politely, remembering a cowboy film he had once seen at the Mu Pakse Cinema. He had anticipated a pageant of pre-technology America conquering its savage frontiers. He had instead watched the star's horse do tricks, and the star sing and play a guitar at a campfire gathering and ultimately shoot revolvers out of the hands of badly shaven criminals. No, thank you. Kiet much preferred *film noir*, Esther Williams musicals, and anything featuring Sydney Greenstreet.

"They're different," said Binh, who had accurately read Kiet's mind. "These are realistic morality plays. You can identify with the marshals and sheriffs. They're not junk; they're classics. They were known in their era as adult westerns."

The offending beggar was back. Kiet saw him squatting on the sidewalk next to the door. Several Caucasian tourists were standing over him, adjusting their lens and shutter settings. Kiet recognized the beggar by his profile—or rather the lack of it.

Luong Burgers' manager, an intense young Luongan in a chocolate brown uniform and a chef's cap, was cocking his head furiously toward the door. Kiet rolled his eyes and replied with a single nod.

He stood, preparing to do his duty, whatever that might be. He remembered the beggar's name. Quoc, a leper with a wooden plug in place of his nose. Quoc had for years begged a subsistence living from foreign visitors who pitied him. While the wretched and diseased homeless were not unknown on Hickorn's streets, his condition was especially horrible.

Quoc was not stupid, however. Of late, he had capitalized on the influx of tourists by offering to have his photograph taken with them. For a pittance one could return home with proof that the squalor of the mysterious Orient had been experienced. Binh thought the practice was disgusting. Kiet regarded it as an opportunity for Quoc to eat. Quoc was on his feet now, a man's arm around him, not quite touching contaminated skin. A woman was snapping pictures.

Kiet and Binh walked to the counter. The manager was ringing up a purchase on a computerized register. The membrane keyboard was laid out like an abacus, each bead in the design of a menu item. Authenticity, Kiet thought.

The manager thanked his customer and turned to the police officers. "He's an eyesore. How can you eat after seeing him?"

"Hickorn's ordinance book is vague on the subject of panhandling," Kiet said. "Unless he assaults someone, he probably is not violating a law."

"These days, more than ever, we have to consider Luong's image, Superintendent," Binh said.

"Image," Kiet muttered.

"Can you please talk to him, gentlemen?" the manager pleaded. "I've received numerous complaints. If he discourages business, I'll lose my job."

"We will," Kiet said. "Come, Captain."

They went outside. The tourists were gone. Quoc was again squatting. He was a tiny, frail man at least Kiet's age. A paper cup beside him contained coins and a few bills. As always, he was grinning for no good reason.

"Quoc, how are you?" Kiet asked.

The beggar's grin widened. "Fine, sir."

The words were garbled and curiously nasal. Kiet remembered that Quoc's condition caused a speech impediment.

He said, "Quoc, there must be other locations as lucrative as this. Please distribute your time between them. If you situate yourself permanently here, I will be forced to continue my investigation and ruin my health by eating bland food. May I suggest departure concourses at the airport? Any complaints will therefore be lodged with travel agents in faraway lands."

Quoc sprang to his feet. "Out of respect for you, Superintendent Kiet, I will."

"What did he say?" Binh asked.

"That he will obey the law whether it exists or not," Kiet translated.

Kiet dropped a fifty-zin coin into his cup. Quoc shook his hand and walked off.

"You're encouraging him, Superintendent," Binh said.

"I gave him—what?—the Luongan counterpart of an American dime."

"Is he really going to the airport?"

Kiet shrugged.

"I intend no disrespect, Superintendent, but that really isn't the way to—"

Binh was interrupted by the loud sputtering of a department motorbike. The patrolman riding it braked hard at the curb, dismounted as if it were on fire, saluted, and handed Kiet a slip of paper.

Kiet read it, took a deep breath, and said, "When?"

"We were notified minutes after you left Headquarters, Superintendent." He was pale and his voice quavered.

"How many know?"

"The officer who received the call, the two remaining at the National Museum awaiting you, the curator, and myself, sir."

"Please return to the museum. Nothing is to be said to anyone. Understand?"

"Yes, sir. Understood." The patrolman started the bike and accelerated into traffic.

"Bad?" Binh asked, knowing that it was.

"Worse than bad," Kiet said. "Worse than worst. The Golden Peacock has been stolen."

2

The Golden Peacock was a secular icon. It was a representation of the feathered headdress worn by Prince Savhana, ancestor of Prince Pakse, in the battle that repelled an invading Chinese army. The year was 154 B.C., the last time the Kingdom of Luong had been victorious in any conflict against outsiders.

The Golden Peacock was not made of feathers and leather bindings, though. It had been fashioned several centuries ago before Luong's gemstone mines played out. Sapphires and rubies mounted on a pure gold armature provided the bird's plumage. More jewels were donated throughout the years. It was at once massive and delicate. In sunlight, the hundreds of gems were so brilliant that people were forced to avert their eyes.

The Golden Peacock was displayed at the National Museum for all but one day of the year. On that day, Prince Pakse, atop an elephant, would accept it in front of the museum and wear it in the parade route that wound through downtown Hickorn and ended at National Stadium.

That day was Savhanakip. On his fingers Kiet ticked off the days from now until then: five. Just five.

What if the Golden Peacock were not recovered and Prince Pakse did not wear it at Savhanakip? he wondered. He erased the image of chaos and rioting before it could vividly form. The Golden Peacock was more than a precious bauble to the Luongan male. It was the symbol of manhood, of vicarious triumph, of North American *machismo*.

That possibility so consumed Kiet that he completely forgot to be terrorized by Binh's maniacal driving. A potential kamikaze when he was merely going to lunch, the young adjutant defied description now as he raced in grim silence between produce carts and pedicabs and shortcutted through alleys surely too narrow for the department's Citroën.

They arrived at the National Museum in minutes. It was located on Mu Savhana, a wide boulevard better known as the Street of Flowers. A rainbow of perennial blooms grew in its median. On each side were rows of grand structures, French legacies that at present housed the National Bank, the National Assembly, and various ministries.

Kiet often thought that Mu Savhana was Hickorn's most beautiful street. But as he got out of the Citroën and gazed at the National Museum's mock pillars and rococo walls, beauty wasn't on his mind. He was contemplating blood and fire.

Two department motorbikes were parked at the entrance. The officers were inside, out of sight. Excellent, Kiet thought. They had good enough sense to be inconspicuous. Everybody would know soon enough.

Kiet and Binh climbed stone steps and pushed through the heavy wood-and-bronze door. Their patrol officers were in the lobby with Dr. Latisa Chi, museum curator.

"Superintendent Kiet. Has it been recovered yet?" Dr. Chi asked in a high-pitched whine.

12

Kiet suppressed a groan. In times of peace, policemen were nuisances best ignored. In times of peril, they were expected to materialize loaves and fishes. "No, Doctor. Please tell me what you can."

Dr. Latisa Chi was a tiny rumpled man with wispy gray hair. He wore thick glasses and a frowning expression of perpetual distraction. Before his appointment to the post of National Museum curator, he had taught history and philosophy at Luong University. Kiet had difficulty dealing with professorial types and he regarded Chi as a hopeless intellectual.

"The museum opens at noon," Dr. Chi said. "I arrived at eleven to prepare. The Golden Peacock was missing."

"Please elaborate, Doctor."

Chi shrugged and wrung his hands. "Alas, the summary is also the text. I came in and discovered that the Peacock was gone."

"Were any of the other exhibits disturbed or stolen?"

"No, not to my knowledge. I was so shaken by . . . by the loss that I haven't inventoried in detail, but cursory inspection tells me nay."

Captain Binh had been conferring with the two officers. "A piece was cut out of a window pane in the rear, by the alley," he reported to Kiet. "The alarm tape on it was bypassed. Apparently the weight-sensitive alarm on the display cover was circumvented too."

"Don't you have a night watchman?" Kiet asked Dr. Chi.

"No. We felt our electronic security measures were adequate. Your police make regular night patrols in the area, so . . ." Dr. Chi's voice trailed off and he shrugged helplessly.

Ah, Kiet mused, so blame is already being assigned. During museum hours, guards monitored for light-fingered tourists, but the night was entrusted to transistors and wires and the Hickorn Police Department. Convenient scapegoats in a matter that would require an abundance of them.

"Come," Kiet said to Binh. "Let's absorb culture."

Kiet looked at everything, taking his time. It had been too long since his last visit anyway. As he progressed he had to admit that Dr. Chi and his staff were doing a wonderful job. Exquisite figurines carved from smuggled Burmese jadeite in the last century by Luongan artisans. Gilded statuary. Stone sculptures of the Buddha. Standing panels of silk and paper depicting virginal ladies in traditional Luongan dresses holding fans. Lacquered bowls. Hammered jewelry. Painting by minor European Post-Impressionists.

And, of course, the centerpiece of the National Museum and, in some respects, of Luong itself, the Golden Peacock. The exhibits were presented in a series of L- and U-shaped alcoves, a clever layout that made each alcove separate and gave the museum an illusion of greater size.

The Golden Peacock had been enshrined in the back, in a rectangular room twice as large as any other exhibition area. It rested on a marble and teak platform, under a glass case. The case was lying off to a side. On a velvet mat in the center of the platform was a circular indentation made by the treasure.

"The alarm on the case is sensitive and in working condition," Binh said. "It is 1960s technology, hardly state-of-the-art, but effective. It's linked to Headquarters and tested weekly."

"When last?" Kiet asked.

"Two days ago," Dr. Chi said.

"Then why did it not sound, please?"

Binh said, "There's a control panel next to the fuse box. The panel cover is bent and scratched. Once inside the building, the thief jimmied it and turned off the alarm switch."

14

"What is there?" Kiet asked, pointing to his right and a door beyond the exhibition entryway.

"The conference room," Dr. Chi said. "We hold lectures and show slides and filmstrips."

Kiet pointed in the opposite direction, to a door beyond the other entrance. "And that way?"

"My office," Dr. Chi said, wiping his perspiring brow with a handkerchief. "The Ministry of Tourism is next to it and behind my office too."

"I recall that wing of the museum being deeper," Kiet said.

"It was. The ministry is growing so rapidly. Office space was deemed a higher priority than the obscure watercolors that hung in that section of the wing."

Kiet remembered the obscure watercolors. They were lovely depictions of riversides and paddies done by contemporary Luongan painters. He shook his head sadly at the thought of clerks replacing art but said nothing.

"Since the tourism campaign began, the National Museum has been subordinate to the ministry, you know," Chi continued. "The museum is such an important facet of the tours. Minister Ridsa is attempting to secure offices across the street. If he is successful, the space will be given back to me."

"Across the street" meant the old United States embassy, Kiet knew. When the Americans moved into their new glass-and-steel monstrosity, they deeded their former quarters to the Kingdom of Luong. Government bureaucracies, forever anxious to expand their paper empires, had descended on the vacated building like vultures on carrion. It was especially prized because of its elevators and central air conditioning. The infighting among ambitious agency heads had become so bitter that His Royal Highness himself would be the final arbiter.

If Kiet were superstitious, he might have believed that his recollection of petty ambition had conjured Minister of

1 5

Tourism Phorn Ridsa. He was not in the least superstitious, but the unpleasant result was the same.

Ridsa came around the corner from his offices and said, "Kiet. Where is it?"

"Loaves and fishes," Kiet muttered.

"What? What are you saying?"

Phorn Ridsa was the antithesis of the bookish Dr. Chi, and the curator seemed to shrink even further in physical comparison. Ridsa was tall, lean, and in his thirties. Kiet reluctantly conceded that he was strikingly handsome. His hair was long, expensively styled, and held in place with a cocoon of hair spray. He wore designer denims, suede shoes, and colorful shirts. He looked to Kiet like a carica-ture of the casually affluent Western tourists his ministry enticed.

Ridsa was a career civil servant. His progress through the ranks was remarkable. Above all else, nepotism ensured success. Most high officials were either close or shirttail relatives of Prince Pakse. Ridsa was the only ministry chief without blood ties. His advancement was attributed to intelligence, which Kiet also conceded, and charm, which he found smarmy. Phorn Ridsa constantly sought the good will of important people. His personal relationships were merely tools, favors granted and favors asked.

Kiet answered Ridsa's question with another. "When did you last see the Golden Peacock, sir?"

"What time was it, Chi? Five or five-fifteen yesterday, I think."

"Yes sir," Dr. Chi said. "People are permitted to browse on their own during normal museum hours. For those desiring greater structure, we schedule two formal tours a day. An Unknown Asia Tours group came at midafter-noon."

"When did the second tour finish?" Kiet asked.

"They should have departed at closing time, four-thirty,"

Chi said. "But Minister Ridsa enjoys conducting slide shows in the conference room when his valuable time permits. He lectured to that second group yesterday and completed his incisive talk shortly after five."

Phorn Ridsa's smile was a smirk. "I have excellent slides of Luong's remote regions. The rugged highlands. The thick jungles of the south. Our guests are prissy, Kiet. They're afraid of venturing out of Hickorn. They're afraid of being bitten by snakes and eaten by tigers in the jungle. They're afraid of being kidnapped in the mountains by opium bandits or communist guerrillas. They relish my tales of terror. Some of the ladies, well, I see them tingle at the mention of the fate the warlord gangs and Rougs guerrillas have in store for captured females."

Kiet was sure Ridsa put on a grand show. He was an articulate and animated speaker, if a bit didactic. "I am certain you are very entertaining, Mr. Minister. Please tell me who closed the museum."

"I did," said Dr. Chi. "I always do. I locked the doors and set the alarms at approximately five-thirty."

"Who has keys?"

Ridsa answered for Chi, speaking loudly. "Chi and myself. What are you trying to say, Kiet?"

Kiet and Ridsa engaged in a staring duel. There were bad feelings between them and there would be no spirit of cooperation in this case or any other. The animosity involved Fop Tia, ex-mayor of Hickorn.

A year ago, Tia had led a counterfeiting operation that nearly destroyed Luong's economy. In conspiracy with an American photocopy machine salesman, he had printed and deluged Hickorn with counterfeit Luongan zin. The zin was impotent prior to the scheme, six hundred of them required to buy a single U.S. dollar on the black market. The flood of phony zin so bloated Hickorn's money supply that inflation raised the ratio to fifteen hundred to one.

Fop Tia's corruption and inefficiency had made him

unpopular, and his reelection prospects were in serious doubt. Tia's initial purpose was to finance that effort, but Kiet flushed him, rendering his political future uncertain. He caught Tia at Hickorn International Airport with an attaché case full of U.S. greenbacks. By then Tia's motivation was greed and escape. Kiet confiscated the money and escorted Tia to his Bangkok flight, in effect putting him in exile.

Phorn Ridsa and Fop Tia were friends, as much as vipers could unite in pure friendship. If their shared visions of power and wealth had not then congealed into a deal, it would have been just a matter of time.

Ridsa blinked, a small victory for Kiet, who said, "No accusations intended, sir. I'm merely trying to establish a fact pattern."

"Fact pattern! You're interrogating Chi and me while the thieves could be melting down the Peacock and selling its gems at this very minute. You should be out on the streets, hunting the bandits down. Kiet, don't you realize what consequences this could have, Savhanakip being less than a week away?"

Kiet felt himself redden. "I have speculated, Mr. Minister. Please, when did you learn of the theft?"

"Chi notified me immediately. I was in my office, but I always enter through the ministry's doors, not the museum's."

Addressing both Chi and Ridsa, Kiet asked, "How many people know thus far?"

"My staff isn't due in until later," Dr. Chi said.

"A couple of my deputy ministers, that's all," Ridsa said.

Roughly ten altogether, Kiet thought. "Rumors and gossip spread in Hickorn like a medieval plague," he said. "We must have secrecy or everyone in the city will know by nightfall."

"Don't patronize me, Kiet. There won't be any leaks at our end. Will there, Chi?"

Dr. Chi shook his head meekly.

"Of course not," Kiet said. "Doctor, I suggest you close the museum until further notice, perhaps for repairs."

"Finally, a constructive idea from you, Kiet," Ridsa said. "Consider it done. Chi, I suggest you fabricate a credible maintenance problem."

Kiet thanked Ridsa and Chi for their assistance, then accompanied Binh on an inspection of the points of forced entry. Binh lingered at the alarm box, obviously troubled.

Kiet swung the panel cover back and forth. The heavy steel plate was scratched and sprung, but the deadbolt lock appeared undamaged. Now he knew why Binh had not been nagging him for permission to assign a forensic team.

Binh's "forensic teams" were a product of his District of Columbia training. He loved to unleash detectives onto a crime scene, with their fingerprint kits and magnifying glasses and vacuum cleaners. Loose barroom talk and informants settling grudges were responsible for solving Luongan crimes, Kiet knew. Not lint encased in microscope slides, not smudged thumbprints. Binh's restraint relieved him. He had feared zealous sleuths smearing fingerprint powder on everything and accidentally knocking over irreplaceable antiquities.

"A key," Kiet said.

"A key," Binh said. "Had to be. Getting in was no sweat. Every pro burglar in town has a glass cutter and knows how to stick a long wire on alarm tape."

"But few are expert locksmiths, are they?"

"No, Superintendent. Our boy had a key to this box. It was an inside job. Had to be."

3

Avenue Alexandre Loubet honored a nineteenth-century French priest who romanized the Luongan language. Chinese-like ideograms of the old written language were incomprehensible to European missionaries, and therefore heathen. The transformation allowed the Christian Bible to be translated more easily into Luongan, thus saving untold souls from eternal damnation.

An important plank of Prince Pakse's foreign policy was the naming and renaming of Hickorn's streets. A year and a half ago, for instance, China committed an obscure diplomatic snub. His Royal Highness retaliated by redesignating Avenue Mao Tse-tung as Avenue Ronald Reagan. The ceremony was elaborate and American foreign aid increased slightly. The supplemental gift of red winter wheat seed would not grow in Luong's climate, but was nonetheless appreciated by farmers, who fed it to their ducks.

Six months later, Ruye Souvanna Phouma was no longer, having been replaced as Rue Chou En-lai. Phouma's Laos posed no threat to Luong's frontiers, and the forgiven

Chinese were once again happy. They rewarded Prince Pakse with a dozen balky tractors and an invitation to visit Beijing.

His Royal Highness, a Roman Catholic, did not tamper with Avenue Alexandre Loubet. Half of Luong shared his faith. The other half were Buddhists. The exchange of religious views had not always been peaceful, and an undercurrent existed that the seventy-eight-year-old monarch was wise not to inflame.

The address of Hickorn Police Headquarters was 900 Avenue Alexandre Loubet. Two stories of blockish stucco, it had served for half a century as a Légionnaire barracks and operations center. Upon independence in 1954, it was relinquished to the natives. The interior remained spare and cold, barely changed from the days of French hegemony.

The place smelled of history. Boots on hallway tile generated echoes. Kiet could almost hear voices—arrogant banter and commands and, toward the end, quieter sounds of relief at being posted in Hickorn instead of Dien Bien Phu. Kiet liked it that way. His headquarters had a businesslike ambience understood by police personnel and criminal guests alike.

Kiet and Binh were in Kiet's office, depressed, wondering what to do next. Binh's gloom was somewhat alleviated by the arrival of a package, which was about the size of Kiet's television carton.

"Our polygraph, Superintendent. I shipped it months and months ago. I thought they'd never get it fixed."

Our polygraph, Kiet thought. The gadget had been a gift of the United States of America. It had been stored unused for lack of need and lack of qualified technicians, tropical heat and humidity assailing its innards like deadly bacteria. It shared storeroom quarters with a ballistics machine and a chemical spectrograph supplied by the Soviets, who were not about to be upstaged.

One day, Binh retrieved it for a particularly vulnerable suspect, a pathological and nervous liar who would surely confess at the mere sight of superior technology. The polygraph's atrophy was compounded by headquarters' wiring, which dated from Kiet's early childhood. Hickorn Metro transmitted erratic electrical current on lines of similar vintage.

Binh plugged in the machine and darkened a four-block radius. Headquarters smelled like burned plastic for a week. Kiet had not scolded him. He meant well and the loss of face, the added shame, would have led to interminable pouting.

This moment was also fragile. "Splendid," Kiet said. "We will have it when we need it. Recent events considered, timing couldn't be better."

Binh began slicing strapping tape. "The polygraph dealer is in Chicago, but it's manufactured in Taiwan. That probably explains the delay. From Hickorn to Chicago. From Chicago to Taiwan. From Taiwan to Chicago. From Chicago to Hickorn. In terms of mileage, it's traveled twice around the world."

Kiet raised a finger. "Please, later. I know your lie revealer will be invaluable in the future, but let's first locate a human subject."

Binh folded his pocketknife and frowned. "Well."

"Unknown Asia Tours Limited," Kiet said. "I know less than I should about the organization."

"Are they really important, Superintendent? We've agreed that there's an extra key, that it was an inside job."

"A tour group was enjoying Minister Ridsa's wisdom and anecdotes after normal closing hours," Kiet reminded him.

"A tourist in collusion with Ridsa or Dr. Chi?"

Kiet shrugged. "Perhaps."

Binh was eyeing his package, a child denied his birthday wish. "If I may be blunt, Superintendent . . ."

"Indeed. Please."

"Well, okay. You've been negative since square one about Unknown Asia Tours. I practically had to drag you into Luong Burgers and you've stubbornly refused to watch your TV. Superintendent, if you have a fault, it's your resistance to change."

"Granted. Guilty as charged."

"Another reason you have less information than you should is that you oppose progress."

"Progress," Kiet said. Binh was entitled to some vengeance for the polygraph-unveiling interruption, but he was becoming bitter and savage. Enough hectoring, enough vengeance. The quota was filled, the books even. "These characters who run Unknown Asia Tours, Captain. From what little I've learned, they're slippery."

"What kind of entrepreneur would bring a financial risk of this magnitude to Luong? Lee Iacocca? Were you expecting Lee Iacocca?"

Kiet was not expecting Lee Iacocca. He had never heard of Lee Iacocca. He said, "Lee Iacocca? Of course not."

"Well," Binh said smugly. "There you are."

"I am where, please?"

Binh threw up his hands and moaned.

"The two Americans who own the concern, I forget their names," Kiet said.

"Charles 'Chick' Chipperfield and Alvin 'Ambulance Al' Selkirk."

"Chipperfield and Selkirk. Yes. They are not candidates for sainthood. Fine. I can live with that. Details, please."

Captain Binh sighed and said, "Chick Chipperfield was a used-car dealer in Seattle."

"United States?"

"Yes, Superintendent, in the American state of Washington. Chipperfield got into trouble with their state attorney general for reversing odometers on automobiles offered for sale on his lot. Selkirk was his brother-in-law and lawyer. Selkirk got him off with a suspended sentence and a

24

negligible fine, but then it was determined that he had falsified documents and bribed a witness. Chipperfield went bankrupt and Selkirk was disbarred."

"Upstanding citizens," Kiet said. "Why is it I have never met either of these gentlemen?"

"They aren't in Hickorn all the time, Superintendent. They have business interests elsewhere. You must have seen Chipperfield, though. He bought Lupien's car. It's gigantic."

"André Lupien? The retired manager of the Michelin rubber plantation?"

"Yes."

Lupien had owned a 1962 Chrysler Imperial, the largest automobile in Luong. "I remember seeing it lately. I didn't look at the driver. I assumed it was old Lupien. But tell me, how did a car salesman and a defrocked lawyer come to create Unknown Asia Tours?"

"The evolution of Unknown Asia Tours is hazy, Superintendent. I do know that Chipperfield and Selkirk were married to sisters who have since divorced them. The sisters operated a Seattle travel agency that specialized in the Orient. I think that while all was well in the marriages the men traveled extensively at reduced cost in this part of the world. They made connections with certain people."

"Including Minister of Tourism Phorn Ridsa?"

"Definitely. They're together constantly when the Americans are in Hickorn."

"Planning Luong's continued progress," Kiet said.

Binh looked at him. "Superintendent, the venture has been a resounding success. Thanks to these men, Hickorn has television, a new cuisine, and a huge increase of tourists who spend their hard currencies in our shops, hotels, and cafés."

Kiet raised his arms in surrender. "All right, Captain. No argument about benefits derived. Are the gentlemen in Hickorn now?"

"I saw the Chrysler yesterday. I'll check."

"One last question, and it is trivial. The origin of their nicknames, Chick and Ambulance Al?"

"Americans are famous for nicknames. I believe Chick is a diminutive, something he was tagged with when he was a boy. Ambulance Al, well, you don't call him that to his face. Ambulance chasing is a disreputable yet quite common aspect of American legal practice. Attorneys aggressively pursue accident victims, hoping to sign them up for representation against insurance companies. If the injury is severe, the settlement can be staggering. The most unscrupulous attorneys will actually follow an ambulance from an accident scene to a hospital and make their pitch if the victim is conscious."

"What if the victim is unconscious or dead?"

"Even better. They wait for loved ones. Juries award millions of dollars when injuries are horrendous."

"Mr. Selkirk raced after ambulances?"

Binh shook his head. "I can't honestly say, but nicknames like that are generally based on behavior. It is an alien concept to us Luongans, isn't it?"

Alien indeed, Kiet thought. If you ran over someone in Hickorn with your bicycle, you replaced his damaged clothing, paid his medical costs, and apologized to his family. If you happened to cripple the poor wretch, you might marry his daughter and take the invalid into your marital household. His compensation would be permanent and fair. There would be no loss of face.

Kiet changed the subject. "What do you believe is being done with our Golden Peacock?"

Binh closed his eyes. "I hate to think it's being desecrated."

"Melted down, as was suggested earlier? Sold piecemeal for intrinsic value?"

"In my opinion, Superintendent, that's vivisection, too terrible to consider."

26

"I agree and I think we can rule it out. Although the eventual sum is mighty, jewels and chunks of gold would have to be sold in a trickle over a period of years. A wealthy collector, perhaps."

"An Arab oil sheik," Binh said. "A reclusive Brazilian billionaire with a private gallery. They say that those types own the majority of disappeared masterpieces, the Leonardos, the Rembrandts."

"The wealthy-collector theory is the easiest for us to deal with," Kiet said. "The only practicable way out of Luong is up. The airport. Otherwise, the thieves would need to travel overland and face the hazards Minister Ridsa narrates in his slide shows."

"I'll have some men assigned to Hickorn International within the hour," Binh said.

"Subtly," Kiet said. The single word was sufficient. Hickorn's customs officials were not known for their integrity, and the Golden Peacock could command a bribe that would temporarily blind any man. Army assistance was out too. To post a company of armed troops would be akin to announcing the crime on loudspeakers.

"Absolutely, Superintendent. I'll select a few of my best and most discreet people. They'll be in plain clothes, strategically situated at concourses and baggage areas. The Peacock is too bulky to be carried out inside a raincoat, you know. Four or five officers will be plenty."

"Splendid. The third possibility is politics."

Binh nodded morosely. "Yeah. It's probably no coincidence the caper went down five days before Savhanakip, is it?"

Binh and the Western slang he brought home from the District of Columbia! Kiet thought. It was as corrupting as his fondness for cheeseburgers. Whatever parallel there was between the Golden Peacock dilemma and the descent of small green buds employed in European cookery escaped him. "No. Who stands to gain?"

"Who with political ambitions doesn't? The communists. Army officers plotting a coup d'état. Civilian bigshots planning a peaceful overthrow, pressuring His Royal Highness into retirement. You name it. If His Royal Highness doesn't wear the Peacock in the parade and is held to blame . . . well."

"True," Kiet said, standing. "Opponents of the monarchy have been quiet lately, perhaps too quiet. We shall see."

Binh left to organize his airport team. Kiet took an urgent message from his desk sergeant. The message was from Ambassador Dang of the Socialist Republic of Vietnam. It was a request that Kiet call on the ambassador at his earliest convenience.

Kiet trudged out to the Citroën. There were occasions when an odious task was preferable to none at all, he thought. The performance of a specific duty as opposed to fretting in limbo. He almost convinced himself that this chore qualified as one of them.

4

The Kingdom of Luong and the Socialist Republic of Vietnam had established diplomatic relations earlier in the year. For their embassy, the Vietnamese rented a modest two-story villa that had stood vacant since the Republic of Korea consulate moved out several months prior. The South Koreans had been in the market for larger quarters anyhow—they bought a mansion in the International District that they felt was a more accurate statement of their economic clout, and fled a despicable address.

The Vietnamese embassy was located on the corner of Rue Ho Chi Minh and Avenue Leonid Brezhnev. The names of two dead Marxists on their letterheads had embarrassed the hysterically anticommunist Koreans. Ambassador Dang of Vietnam regarded the address as providential.

The embassy anteroom was ill lighted and decorated with only the nation's flag and a large photograph of Ho Chi Minh. It smelled of fish sauce and intrigue. A sullen guard motioned Kiet upstairs to Ambassador Dang's office, where the environment was cheerier, but just as politically severe.

On pastel walls hung portraits of various heroes—Lenin, Marx, Stalin, Vo Nguyen Giap, Pham Van Dang, and, behind Ambassador Dang, a fantastical illustration that depicted Uncle Ho shooting down a B-52 bomber with a rifle.

Dang rose from his desk, greeted Kiet with a restrained smile and a moist handshake, and gestured for him to sit. "Superintendent Kiet, so nice that you could see me immediately."

Bamsan Kiet sat. The vinyl-and-chrome chair in front of Dang's desk was low slung and extremely uncomfortable. Kiet's knees were at chest level and his buttocks nearly touched the carpeting. The room contains a dozen conventional chairs, and this is always the one reserved for me, he thought. Dang's ego had outgrown his body. He could not bear to look upward at an inferior. Now their eye contact could be perfectly parallel to the surface of the planet.

Dang puzzled Kiet in other ways. He was thirty years old, five feet tall, balding, and moon faced. He wore tailored pinstripes, complete with vest. His nails were manicured and he spoke seven languages. His circumference equaled his height.

Kiet's preconception of the top representative of the region's military menace had been of a grizzled old soldier who lugged artillery pieces up the hills surrounding Dien Bien Phu, a stolid guerrilla whose sacrifice helped bid farewell to France's Asian empire. After the 1975 victory, the Socialist Republic of Vietnam had rewarded revolutionary loyalty and little else.

Kiet intensely distrusted Ambassador Dang. It was nothing personal. The man simply did not belong.

"Thank you, Mr. Ambassador. How may I be of service?"

Dang waited to reply until he lighted a cigarette from the one he was smoking. He chain-smoked Salems, a mentholated American type. Another contradiction, Kiet thought; a counterrevolutionary brand preference.

"Soccer arrangements. I apologize for being a pest."

Every year, the Savhanakip parade culminated at National Stadium, where a match was played between Luong's national team and a foreign squad.

Kiet said, "We are prepared for their arrival in three days. Has the itinerary changed?"

"Oh, no," Dang said, exhaling smoke. "One of my faults is fussiness. I am obsessed with pre-planning. Every tiny item must be worked out or I cannot sleep. I'm a worry-wart."

Kiet silently agreed, then said, "I will have twenty men at the airport for their arrival, Mr. Ambassador. A motorcade will bring the team directly here. Officers will be posted outside day and night. Any excursions team members wish to take will be heavily escorted too."

Dang shook his head. Jowls quivered. "No. With the exception of an evening out for dinner, there will be no sightseeing. They are coming to play soccer, not to gape in your decadent shops. Do not take this as a criticism of your efficiency, Superintendent Kiet, but no degree of security can anticipate every contingency."

Kiet translated *contingency* into *defection*, a fear by Dang that athletes of his socialist paradise might maneuver to miss their homeward flight. "I assure you, sir, we will be thorough."

"Oh, of course you will." Dang chuckled, inhaled smoke, and wheezed. He patted his midsection. "I love soccer, but I don't have the physique for it. This is our national team's first match outside of Vietnam, you know."

Kiet knew. How many times had Dang reminded him? What was he getting at? "The Kingdom of Luong is highly honored, Mr. Ambassador."

"We reciprocate the esteem by permitting our team to contribute to your Savhanakip holiday. Joining in diplomatic relations made Prince Pakse unpopular with a reac-

31

tionary bully. His kind and brotherly gesture of solidarity enraged them. I applaud his courage."

Further translations. *Reactionary bully*: the United States. *Kind and brotherly gesture of solidarity*: renaming a street on the fringe of downtown Avenue Vo Nguyen Giap, in tribute to the general who had commanded the wars of liberation against France and America.

"Luong is neutral," Kiet said evenly, concealing his impatience.

"Neutral *and* permissive," Dang said, tapping a chubby finger on his desktop for emphasis. "An archaic monarchy, if you will excuse my bluntness. Money and materialism are opiates, you know. They dull the senses of your oppressed masses. Terrorism thrives in the absence of heightened consciousness and a class struggle."

Kiet thought it was the other way around, the turmoil of power plays bringing bomb throwers out from under rocks. "Terrorism does *not* thrive in Hickorn, Mr. Ambassador. I am working hard to ensure that an anarchist doesn't harm your soccer players."

Dang smiled condescendingly. "Of course you are, Superintendent, and I have confidence in your abilities. You are justifiably cross with me. I apologize. The game, the joyous purity and competition of sport, how sad it is that we cannot divorce political considerations."

How do you separate soccer at the national level and politics? Kiet wondered. Luong fielded a weak team. Savhanakip opponents were picked on the basis of poor showings in World Cup group play The last two invitees, Nepal and Brunai, had been crushed by so-so Hong Kong and Malaysian squads, eliminated early. Their ineptitude was encouraging. But they defeated Luong 4–0 and 5–0, respectively.

His Royal Highness' passion was pocket billiards, but he loved all sports and ached for a Savhanakip soccer victory. The last had been in 1971, against a Macau team decimated by an intestinal virus. The Vietnamese were untested against international competition, thus a logical choice.

For Vietnam's part, Luong was the softest prey available. International soccer success meant prestige, instant respectability.

So there it was. Each country had measured the other as quarry. The symbiosis of soccer and politics, a flash of national pride. Kiet hoped that it didn't explode in anyone's face like a cheap firecracker.

"I look forward to attending the game," he said.

"As do I. Asian versus Asian," Dang said. "We're brothers in skin and soul, comrades in heritage, comrades in the struggle against Western imperialism. The outcome is unimportant. We'll figuratively embrace afterward, our bond strengthened."

Brothers in skin and soul? Racial animosity between Luongans and Vietnamese began centuries before either laid eyes on a blond, milk-skinned Frenchman. Kiet felt queasy. Clichés affected him like spoiled food. "Yes. Stronger."

"Self-determination, Superintendent Kiet," Dang went on. "It is the essence of political consciousness, don't you think?"

"Certainly."

"How many Americans are permanently in Luong?"

"Three or four hundred," Kiet said. "Why?"

Dang licked his lips and frowned. "So few in number, but able to make your leaders act like them, to act like puppets."

Had the man summoned him here to deliberately offend him? Kiet retaliated in a pleasant voice. "What is it you call the *thousands* of Soviet advisers in Vietnam, Mr. Ambassador?"

"Beg pardon?"

"Americans without dollars, is it not?"

"Oh, yes, I have heard that."

"An affectionate term, I'm sure," Kiet said.

Dang clapped his hands together and grinned, startling Kiet. "That is my precise point. Despite our sincere efforts, our societies remain imperfect. Neither of us can completely avoid contamination and mischief. We are intelligent men and understand this. Accordingly, I trust that you will be receptive to an idea I have that will increase our security readiness."

"Excuse me?"

Ambassador Dang pushed a button on his intercom. "The appointment of a liaison to assist you and your police department in protecting our soccer team."

"A liaison?"

"A person who will work directly with you and coordinate with us."

"I always appreciate extra manpower," Kiet lied.

"She is capable and dedicated, Superintendent Kiet."

"She?"

"Madame Mai Le Trung is new to Luong. She is my cultural attaché, but her experience is varied. She fought the Yankees and the Thieu regime puppets. Her husband was a regimental commander who died at Hue during the Tet Offensive of 1968."

Kiet took a deep breath. He visualized a leathery beast, bandoliers draped over her black pajamas. "Splendid credentials," he said.

The door opened behind him. Kiet and Dang rose to their feet. A woman entered and bowed slightly. She wore the traditional Vietnamese *áo dài*, a silken tunic that flowed over pants and blouse. Her hair was tied at the back and reached her waist; Kiet doubted that it had been cut since North Vietnamese tanks rumbled into Saigon in 1975. Her face was taut but not in the least leathery. Her eyes were wide-set, her features delicate. Her breasts were unusually ample for an Asian. She had to be in her forties, but looked younger. Though she remained quietly, respectfully still, she broadcast energy and robust health. The woman was beautiful.

"Superintendent of Police Bamsan Kiet, may I introduce Madame Mai Le Trung."

Her handshake was firm yet feminine, as dry as Dang's was wet. "I am eager to cooperate with you, Superintendent," she said. "I know I will learn much about police security procedures."

"Among other duties mutually agreed upon, Madame Mai can serve as your interpreter," Dang said. "Her melodious voice should tell you that she speaks fluent Luongan."

"A welcome addition to my security team," Kiet said, addressing them both.

"May I contact you at your convenience to discuss arrangements?" Mai asked Kiet.

"Uh, certainly."

"Good," Dang said, lighting a Salem and turning to a stack of documents. "I'll leave the specifics to you extraordinary people. Kiet, your flexibility has relieved a tremendous burden from my shoulders."

Mai shook Kiet's hand, bowed, and left.

Kiet walked outside, dazed. His nausea had passed, replaced by a headache. He sat in his car for a moment and thought.

Ambassador Dang had hoodwinked him. His pompous baiting caused Kiet to strike back with a snide reference to his Bolshevik masters. Dang's trap was set. He admitted a flaw in his socialist paradise and likened it to Luong's. Kiet's political consciousness revealed this alarming similarity. Dang had lost face.

Kiet could not refuse Dang's "liaison" notion. To do so would inflame the insult. To do so in the face of logic would indicate obstinacy, if not stupidity. Kiet would lose face.

He started the Citroën and smiled. Dang. Perhaps the

rotund fellow never crawled under barbed wire to cut a throat, but he was as stealthy as any fanatical guerrilla. In Kiet's opinion, diplomacy and cunning were synonymous. Ambassador Dang *belonged*.

5

Kiet swallowed an aspirin tablet and drove to Unknown Asia Tours Ltd. Dang and his diplomat's logic had given him the headache. Perhaps medicine and detective's logic would relieve it. Unknown Asia Tours was the conspicuous variable in this mess, possibly the common denominator.

Never before had the Golden Peacock fluttered its priceless plumage and flown out of the National Museum. Not until now and the greedy tourism craze. Ergo, a connection, albeit a logically shaky one. But Kiet had nothing better to do than feel sorry for himself.

The tourist enterprise and its television station operated in a shop purchased from the Vai Tuoi Electrical Generator Works. Vai Tuoi, the founder, had repaired and overhauled automotive and industrial generators since the mid-1920s. The firm prospered under Tuoi's sons and his sons' sons. The latter sons and their spouses proved inexplicably barren. In ten or fifteen years the family business would wither like their failed seeds. The prospect was humiliating and by all accounts the buyers had paid a generous price, attracted by ample square footage and heavy-duty circuits.

They were located on Mu Pakse, a block east of the Hickorn Continental Hotel. The modest wooden VAI TUOI sign above the door had been replaced with neon: UAT * CHANNEL 7-TV LUONG. Stucco and trim were painted in vivid yellow and green. Captain Binh had praised the redecoration as "nifty" and "trendy." Bamsan Kiet was less enthusiastic, believing that bright colors were suitable for birds, not business establishments.

He walked in on a dozen American and Japanese tourists. Some were seated, some were standing at the tourist information window. Most were studying maps and brochures. None were smiling. The agent on duty was telling a man that she would try to substitute a trip to the National Assembly. The man replied with a grimace usually reserved for foul odors.

The agent was a comely young woman named Lin Aidit. She had been a Ministry of Tourism employee for five or six years. Kiet knew her from the days when the majority of her clients were travelers trapped in Hickorn after their stopover flights were canceled or delayed. She wore a harried expression and a uniform that was unfortunately the same yellow and green as the outside walls.

"Superintendent Kiet," she asked, sighing, "have you heard about the National Museum?"

"Heard what?"

"That it's shut down for repairs."

"Yes. Leaking water pipes. The floors are drenched."

Her eyebrows raised. "Pipes? Dr. Chi informed me that rats gnawed through wiring."

"Uh, that too," Kiet said. "A burst pipe sent them into a chewing frenzy. It will take days to repair the damage."

She waited for her dissatisfied customer to take a seat, then said, "I have to find activities for this group tomorrow. The National Assembly is so boring. They debate for hours and hours about nothing, but I can't think of an alternative on short notice."

"Our parliamentary system can be fascinating," Kiet said without conviction.

"Could we speak alone for a minute, sir?" Lin Aidit released a swinging door at the counter and led Kiet to a glassed-in cubicle, where she whispered, "A horrible rumor is circulating."

"What rumor?"

"That the Golden Peacock was stolen. It *can't* be true, can it?"

Kiet avoided her eyes and forced a smile that strained his cheeks. "Where on earth did you hear that wild story, Lin?"

"On the corner. I bought a pastry and the vendor told me."

Hickorn's gossip telegraph, Kiet thought. Food cart vendors, beggars, bartenders, sidewalk peddlers, pimps, moneychangers, pedicab drivers—every tidbit that initiated at the top of the pyramid, whether true or false, instantly fell to the bottom and seeped upward. An osmosis unique to Hickorn.

"The man is demented," Kiet said.

"I am relieved. We have quadruple our usual bookings. They've come for Savhanakip. I'm pleased that there's no trouble."

Kiet flicked a wrist, as if launching a piece of lint. He hoped the gesture appeared casually honest. "No trouble. None. The Peacock is safe from flooding, rats, and burglars."

"I *am* relieved. I must say, Superintendent, that I feared you were bearing bad news."

"Police officers don't necessarily bear bad news."

"But to my knowledge you have never been to Unknown Asia Tours. They say that you are hostile to television and the tourism expansion."

"They?"

39

"Binh is a friend of mine," Lin Aidit said, blushing.

Kiet wasn't surprised. Captain Binh had an enviable string of girl friends. "No. I am just curious, unfamiliar with the technology of television transmission. Binh says I resist progress. I am attempting to prove him wrong."

"My pleasure, sir. Allow me," Lin Aidit said, taking Kiet through a door. In a room that was incredibly hot, three technicians were monitoring switches and dials on electronic panels. They wore only shorts and sandals. Perspiration gleamed on them. Next to the panels were two man-high cameras on castered carriages. The cameras seemed to be decommissioned, cords tied up in careful bundles, their lenses angled toward one another.

"Cross-eyed," Kiet said, pointing.

Lin Aidit laughed. "Now that you mention it, I see. The cameras are inactive until live telecasting starts. I don't know when that will be. We're playing old American westerns and they're becoming extremely popular."

"Westerns," Kiet muttered. "Cowboys."

"I *love* them, especially 'Have Gun, Will Travel.' Which is your favorite?"

Kiet dodged the question. "Why is it so hot?"

"Vacuum tubes. The machinery is very, very old. It was manufactured before microchips and transistors. Mr. Chipperfield and Mr. Selkirk acquired it from a public broadcasting station in South Dakota. They were changing over to modern color equipment."

"The neon sign. The Channel Seven," Kiet said. "Where, please, are channels one, two, three, four, five, and six?"

"Weren't you given a complimentary set, Superintendent? I'd be shocked if you'd been overlooked."

"Yes. Yes I was."

"The TVs have settings for channels two through thirteen. The station has to give the viewer a number to tune in."

"Why seven?"

40

"An arbitrary choice. Dr. Chi suggested it at a meeting. He said seven is considered a lucky number in some cultures."

"Interesting and informative," Kiet said, wiping his forehead with his handkerchief. "How is it going for you, Lin? In general?"

"Busy," she said with a sigh. "I run the office and lead tours too. The old times weren't as exciting."

Kiet detected sarcasm. "Aren't Mr. Selkirk and Mr. Chipperfield directly involved?"

"Hah," she said sharply. "When one or the other is in town, they come in and tell me to do this and do that. Then they disappear. That's how they're directly involved."

"I understand that they are seldom in Hickorn."

"Very, very seldom. The two of them at once, hah, that is the rarest of the rare. Yesterday *and* today I had the privilege of seeing them. It's been weeks. I can't tell you what a thrill it is to receive advice and orders from them simultaneously."

"I would like to meet the gentlemen."

"Go to the Continental, Superintendent. You may find them."

"They stay there?"

"Where else?" Lin Aidit said in exasperation. "I'll see them later. I know I will. They'll drink on the *terrasse* and think of more excellent advice for me."

"Where else indeed," Kiet said. "I regret that I cannot relieve your work burden. Are there other matters that require my department's assistance?"

"No. A small fraction of my tourists make silly demands and whine, but they behave. Oh, well, I . . . no."

"What, please?"

"Do you have influence or control over the Postal Office?"

"Sadly, no. Are you receiving complaints?"

"I am. Our guests mail postcards on arrival day and

41

the postcards don't get to their homes until weeks after they do. The bulk of the complaint letters concern mail delivery."

Kiet nodded in sympathy. Early in the century, the Luong Postal Service began life as a duplicative mandarin bureaucracy. The French added extra layers of supervisors and clerks. Following Independence, Luongan postal managers continued in the spirit of providing employment for every unemployable friend and relative capable of rubber stamping and initialing a piece of mail. It was said that a letter posted at a downtown hotel took as long to reach an outgoing airplane at Hickorn as it would to be hand carried to Greenland.

Kiet shrugged. "Sorry, I can't jail anyone for incompetence."

Lin Aidit smiled a weary smile. "No miracles for me on the mail, Superintendent? Maybe you can offer an improvement on my National Assembly plan for this group?"

Kiet patted his stomach. "Feed them. Everybody loves to eat. Luong Burgers?"

Lin Aidit's face contorted. "Yucch!"

6

Kiet stepped out of Unknown Asia Tours Ltd.'s television control studio and found the drop in temperature to one hundred degrees Fahrenheit unrefreshing. Ninety degrees, splendid; one hundred and beyond, no, thank you. It was late afternoon and his stomach was rumbling. The starch and grease in his Luong Burgers cheeseburger deluxe, French fries, and rare tropical fruit milkshake had satisfied fleetingly. No staying power in Western cuisine, he decided; you eat and before you know it, you're famished again.

Siesta time was winding down. Within the hour, the streets and sidewalks would once again be clogged with buyers and sellers haggling noisily over prices of produce, meats, jewelry, appliances, and clothing; with bicycles, pedicabs, and automobiles blithely imperiling one another; with pedestrians who browsed, ate and drank, sought lovers, chatted with friends and strangers, shoplifted, and wandered in search of the answer to boredom. For the present, though, Hickorn was dead.

At siesta, anybody with a brain hastened indoors to

43

escape the heat. Bamsan Kiet and his police department did not, could not. Criminals would take advantage of the city's torpor and capitalize like looters during a catastrophe.

Kiet looked at heat waves warping the air above his Citroën's roof and chose to walk. The Continental was just a block and a half away, but the sun was dead center in the sky, searing shadows from the pavement. His alternatives were to roast or to fry.

Under his breath, Kiet cursed the irony of Hickorn traffic's being safe only when it was unbearable to drive. Sit behind the wheel of your automobile at siesta and the upholstery would bond to your skin. He walked fast, perspiration-soaked handkerchief held to his head protecting a thinning scalp. He was tired and hungry. Triple-digit temperatures made him grumpy, but they didn't affect his appetite.

The Hickorn Continental was Luong's finest hotel. Built sixty years ago by Frenchmen and owned to this day by their absentee descendants, it boasted what travel pamphlets termed a "sleepy colonial ambience." The ground level was open-air except for pillars that supported three floors of guest rooms. This was the *terrasse*, a restaurant and bar and unholy rendezvous point. Throughout the years, generations of dreamers and hustlers had whispered their deals, sipping aperitifs and lying in twenty languages. Kiet wondered in moments of whimsy whether Galileo would have insisted that the Earth was not the center of the universe if the *terrasse* had then existed.

Kiet had no trouble locating a table underneath a ceiling fan. Four of every five tables were vacant. He slumped into a chair, uninterested in seedy historical speculation. His needs were food, drink, and information.

He scanned a menu. It was new. It did not look right, did not feel right. The paper was sealed in clear plastic, the cover page printed in Unknown Asia Tours' damnably vivid yellows and greens. He thumbed through it to poultry, craving, because of the heat, a fare lighter than his customary fried shrimp. He read the selections and groaned.

A waiter appeared and poured a glass of ice water.

"Hello," he said, beaming. "My name is Tho. I will be your server today."

Kiet studied him. A pinned-on nameplate indeed confirmed that he was Tho. He wore black slacks, white shirt, black bow tie, and red vest. *Terrasse* waiters dressed informally and kept a deferential distance from diners. Who was this aggressive young man who was practically in his lap?

"Sir, may I recommend the beef medallions? Our chef carved them from exquisitely tender hindquarters and will grill them to order over mesquite—"

"No, thank you, Tho. A Golden Tiger for the time being, please."

Tho maintained his beaming good cheer, said yes, sir, and scurried off for the beer. Kiet spotted the hotel manager, Gaston LaCroix, and waved him over.

"A wonderful surprise, Superintendent," he said with a jittery smile.

"Join me, LaCroix. We have to talk."

LaCroix was an antique, an expatriate who had clerked for the last French governor-general, married a Luongan woman, and stayed on after Independence. He was pale and thin, dressed as always in a white suit. Because of his attire, LaCroix struck Kiet as an emaciated facsimile of Kiet's favorite Western actor, Sydney Greenstreet.

Kiet tapped the menu. "Where, please, is the roast pigeon?"

"I was compelled to eliminate it, Superintendent. One evening, a tourist lady fell ill."

"The pigeon was rank?"

"No. It was fresh and wonderfully prepared," LaCroix said. "We served the complete bird, as you know."

"How else would you?"

"That is the inexplicable thing. She claimed the sight of the neck and head made her sick. She claimed the eyes stared at her. She vomited on her Dior pants suit. Can you conceive the influence on the evening's dinner trade? Can you conceive my chef's loss of face? These squeamish tourists, I don't know what complaint will befall me next. Our fish entrées are being prepared headless too because of the incident."

"These substitutions," Kiet said. "Skinless and boneless chicken breasts, broiled and accompanied by peculiar sauces."

LaCroix threw up bony hands. "Peculiar sauces for peculiar tastes, Superintendent. I must adapt. I must import frozen breasts. A Luongan-grown chicken breast is too small for a satisfactory meal."

Kiet closed the menu. "I'll have the one with the Oregon raspberries, I suppose. Whatever an Oregon raspberry is."

"The dish will pleasantly surprise you, Superintendent. My chef has creatively adapted, although he hasn't spoken to me in days."

Tho, Kiet's server, returned with a chilled Golden Tiger. LaCroix barked Kiet's order and snapped his fingers. Tho sprinted to the kitchen. "They also demand hyperactive waiters," LaCroix said apologetically.

The ceiling fan was shoveling air about in tepid slabs, providing not even psychological relief. Kiet drank half the bottle. He felt better, a little better. He said, "LaCroix, aside from food—"

"The rumor, yes. Is it true?"

"No," Kiet said.

"Are you reading my mind, Superintendent? The Golden—"

"No. Disregard any gossip and rumors but the variety

46

I'm asking you to relay to me. You have a hotel guest named Selkirk and a hotel guest named Chipperfield."

"Exceptional gentlemen," LaCroix said, sucking yellowed dentures. "They are technically to blame for the roast pigeon travesty, but I'm not criticizing. The benefits of Unknown Asia Tours outweigh nominal adjustments to the tastes of our clientele."

"Increased clientele," Kiet said.

LaCroix showed his porcelain teeth. "I have no vacancies. I am booked weeks in advance. The television sets, a fantastic addition! My guests can retreat to their rooms at siesta and if they do not sleep or make love, they can tune in an exciting slice of frontier America."

LaCroix glanced at his watch. "As timing would have it, Superintendent, 'The Rifleman' is on in seven minutes. That man and his trick rifle and his son confronting those scoundrels! Do you like the series?"

"Yes. A splendid show," Kiet said. "I trust I will not detain you. Two favors, please. Describe Mr. Selkirk and Mr. Chipperfield. I need to interview them. And as circumstances permit, observe the exceptional gentlemen and report anything shady to me and me alone."

"Superintendent, the privacy of my guests is sacrosanct. I do not pry."

Kiet finished his Golden Tiger in a prolonged sip. "Do your accountants in Paris know that your gift televisions have coin slots? And does Hickorn's ordinance book require taxes paid on the coins? I know I'm overly curious, but I cannot help it. We detectives are compulsive investigators."

LaCroix fidgeted. Tho, Kiet's server, pounced, bearing a fresh beer. Kiet drank, glaring at the Frenchman. They had played this game for years. In Kiet's thirteen years as superintendent he had not once stumbled upon LaCroix's constant embezzlements, nor had he observed *terrasse* "hostesses," young lovelies in slit Suzy Wong dresses,

47

losing their way between the bar and their tables, to drift confusedly upstairs a minute or so ahead of their male patrons.

Kiet's myopia never cost LaCroix money. The price was information. Kiet billed him infrequently, but when he did it was payment on demand. "You have Hickorn's widest eyes and ears, Monsieur."

"What should be regarded as shady?"

"I don't know, LaCroix, but you will. The description, please."

"See for yourself," LaCroix said, shooting a jerky arm toward a table on the Rue Ho Chi Minh side.

Two middle-aged Caucasians shared it and a pitcher of clear liquor. They were drinking from stemmed glasses.

"Them?"

LaCroix's eyes were on his watch. "Them. They are princes, Superintendent. I don't know the reason for your interest and I'm loath to lecture you on how to do your job, but your asking me to spy on these gentlemen, I fear, is a waste of your valuable time."

"Thank you for not lecturing," Kiet said. "And remember the monkeys, LaCroix. See evil, hear evil, speak evil. Speak it to me and nobody else."

"Superintendent, isn't it the reverse?"

"Your television show awaits, LaCroix."

LaCroix got up, told Kiet to enjoy his meal, and hurried in a mincing, arthritic pace to his cowboys. Tho arrived instantaneously with a plate of hot food. Kiet did enjoy his meal, though the chicken, rice, and vegetables were a trifle mild and textureless. Nic sau corrected the chicken's blandness. The raspberry glaze was surprisingly tasty.

As Kiet ate, he watched Chipperfield and Selkirk drink and converse in hushed tones. Each man was similar to Kiet in height and girth, average for Caucasians, stocky and tall for Luongans. He pegged their ages as a year or two apart—early to middle forties. One had a full head of graying, tightly curled hair. His skin was darkly tanned, evidence of the odd Western compulsion to intentionally expose one's self to the sun. The other's hair was reddish and wispy, trimmed long and combed back. His complexion was ruddy, evidence of prolonged exposure to alcoholic beverages. Gray Hair was clothed conventionally in dark slacks and white shirt. Red Hair obeyed a fashion that may well have been extraterrestrial: maroon and white checked trousers, white shirt with bold green stripes, white patent leather belt and shoes.

Kiet finished his meal, ordered a third Golden Tiger, paid his check, walked to the exceptional gentlemen, and introduced himself.

Gray Hair rose and shook his hand vigorously. "Alvin Selkirk," he said, of course omitting the Ambulance Al sobriquet. "You're the police chief, right? The name rings a bell. My pleasure."

"Police superintendent," Kiet said.

"Chick Chipperfield," said Red Hair, who did not bother to stand. "Take a load off."

Kiet interpreted the remark as an invitation to sit, so he did. Chipperfield lifted the pitcher and asked, "How 'bout a martini? It's drier than a nun's you-know-what. That Amber Death'll rot your innards."

In Kiet's opinion, Luongan Golden Tiger was as velvety smooth as a brew could be. Westerners had tagged it Amber Death and this was forever puzzling. "Gin? No. My beer is fine."

"Different strokes," Chipperfield said, shrugging. "Okay, fine."

"I dabbled in criminal law in the States," Selkirk said. "My relationship with the police was on a primarily business basis. I can count social calls on the fingers of one hand."

Luongan attorneys had also perfected the annoying art of probing without actually asking questions, Kiet thought.

49

He said, "Whether this is a social call depends on the development of the conversation. Social to social, yes. Social to antisocial, no."

Chipperfield winked. "Slick answer. I like it."

Selkirk shook his shirtfront, coaxing a breeze. "Except for it being hotter than Hades, this isn't a bad interrogation situation."

"A routine inquiry, gentlemen. Tell me, please, what you have done and where you have been during the past twenty-four hours."

"Okay, fine. We're in the travel business," Chipperfield said. "Itineraries are second nature to yours truly and his faithful companion, *kemo sabey*. Lemme see. High noon, yesterday, touched down outta Bangkok. Did lunch. Saw our boy Ridsa. Went to our shop. That's UAT, Unknown Asia Tours. Dinner, a toddy or three, beddie-bye time. Up with the roosters. Scouted different tour possibilities. The Ma San River is like a bucket of warm piss. We're thinking gondolas. Back to the shop, UAT. Jacked up the hired help. Went over some figures. Short snooze. The here and now."

Chipperfield's rapid-fire slang would challenge Captain Binh's translation abilities, Kiet thought, but innocence seemed to be the prevailing theme. "A busy itinerary, economically stated," he said.

"Old Yellow cuts a swath. We tool through town in style. And fast," Chipperfield said. "Your Hickorn traffic is a Chinese fire drill, but when they see Yellow they part like the Red Sea. I know cars. I used to sell them. You couldn't give me a piece of that Jap tin they roll out of the factories these days. Yellow's got some material in her. Forty-eight hundred pounds of sweet ride."

Kiet peered past a pillar to the 1962 Chrysler Imperial, which was parked a block north. It devoured two spaces and the majority of a third. Polished chromium and custard paint glistened. Racing around its circumference, he mused, could be an Olympic event. He said, "Traveling at such breakneck speed, you may have forgotten to mention a stop, a footnote in your busy itinerary."

"Where should we not have been, Superintendent? Where are you accusing us of being?" Selkirk replied quickly. "Isn't that the bottom line?"

Kiet was tempted to blurt "National Museum" but he realized he didn't have to. "Were you somewhere you should not have been?"

"You'll have to tell me where that is, Superintendent," Selkirk said. "We haven't the foggiest. Do we, Chick?"

"Uh-uh. No way, José."

The Golden Peacock rumor had doubtlessly spread to every Hickornian not in a hospital coma ward or a cremation urn, yet the exceptional gentlemen had not repeated it. Nor had they bemoaned the National Museum closure, a major inconvenience to Unknown Asia Tours. They *knew*.

"If you don't know where you shouldn't have been," Kiet said, "it follows that you weren't there."

"It does," Selkirk said. "It does."

Chipperfield looked at Kiet and said, "You know, you fuckers really are inscrutable."

7

Kiet abbreviated his interview with
Chipperfield and Selkirk and went home. Prolonged chitchat would have been a waste of time. The pair were so
innocent they were virginal. Captain Binh had an American saying for that, a metaphor based on the erection of a
stone wall. Besides, Kiet had accomplished one of his
goals, the announcement of suspicion. He believed that no
matter how vague and undocumented a suspicion, the
specter of a police officer behind one's shoulder tended to
generate anxiety, tended to prompt unpredictable behavior. A stop at Headquarters would be equally senseless. If
Binh had made any progress he would have tracked Kiet
down.

Bamsan Kiet lived in a modest four-room home. It was
prosperous by Hickorn standards, but no object of envy to
moneyed Luongans and foreigners who resided in the
International District. The small surrounding courtyard
had been walled with concrete and wrought-iron spikes by
the builder, a paranoiac Frenchman in the colonial civil
service. This barrier generously defined the dwelling as a

villa. Kiet had lived there alone since Tien, his beloved wife, perished in the cholera epidemic of 1966.

Alone but for a stray tomcat who had adopted him several years ago, Kiet was reminded, as he entered and saw the obese animal asleep atop the television carton. The cat was spoiled, arrogant, and responded to affection only when it was hungry. It treated its master like an inefficient manservant. Kiet punished his selfish indifference by refusing to name him.

"Off. Off. Let's slop in our trough," Kiet said, placing the cat by his food bowl. "They nag me about hating progress. I shall prove that I am as progressive as any other fool. I shall experience the miracle of television."

The cat sniffed at the bowl and glowered at Kiet.

"Table scraps, cat. What I eat," Kiet explained. "Whose fault is it that the food has gone stale? And why am I talking to you? Yes, don't tell me. It's the beer. No sane and sober man would converse with a stupid beast."

The cat meowed.

"All right, damn you, all right." Kiet discarded the scraps and poured milk into the bowl. "No need for obscenities."

The cat slurped loudly, temporarily appeased.

"Thank you. You are welcome," Kiet muttered. He removed the television receiver from the carton, put it on a living room table, plugged it in, extended the antenna, and pulled the On switch.

A steady and grating rasp emanated from the speaker. On the screen were white, gray, and black dots that danced like Java pepper being shaken in a tray.

Kiet's headache had reemerged. Golden Tiger's transition from mild intoxication to hangover was remarkably swift. He groaned, vowed again to someday cease drinking in the daytime, and went to the refrigerator for a bottle of analgesic. He returned, took a long swig of Golden Tiger, and remembered Lin Aidit speaking of Dr. Chi's lucky number.

He clicked the tuning knob to 7. Raspy noise became Latin music. Beginning credits scrolled. Two excellent Mexican horsemen, one handsome and heroic, the other fat and silly, neutralized a band of obnoxious criminals within thirty minutes. The handsome and heroic Mexican stole a chaste kiss from a senorita and mounted his horse. The fat and silly one reacted by saying, "Oh, Ceesco!"

Then came a second avenging team of splendid horsemen, a masked Caucasian and an indigenous American who wore fringed leather and coincidentally addressed the Caucasian as *kemo sabey*, just as Chick Chipperfield had addressed Ambulance Al Selkirk. Their adversaries were also moral and physical inferiors. At the conclusion, the heroic Caucasian kissed nobody. He and the native rode toward a sunset, shouting "Hi-ho Silver, away!" as a citizen of the settlement they had saved examined a memento, a silver bullet.

All dialogue was dubbed in one-voice Luongan, but monotone delivery did not diminish the action, the excitement. Kiet liked what he had seen, he liked it very much. Antisocial types were handed their comeuppance and removed from honest society. No one was killed or seriously wounded. The worst injuries were to the hands of criminals, whose guns were shot out of them. The fast resolution and retribution appealed immensely.

Kiet also liked the concept of chief law enforcer and sidekick, although he could not quite identify Binh and himself with those characters. Binh would rightfully be insulted if compared to Pancho, and Kiet had reservations about Cisco. Any Hickorn male strutting in decoratively stitched clothing was a sissy boy and that was that.

While the Lone Ranger was closer to the ideal, clothing remained a problem. The paunchy and conservative Kiet would never wear such a tight costume. His young adjutant and Tonto did not mesh either. The Indian was preferable to Pancho, and he did an impressive share of the crimebusting, but in his grunting passivity he sharply contrasted with the articulate and energetic Binh.

Two episodes of "Gunsmoke" followed, back to back. Kiet was so infatuated by the star that he dismissed sidekick requirements. If Chester's gimpy leg and whiny demeanor insulted Binh, so be it. This was Marshal Matt Dillon's show anyway, a show as harshly realistic as "The Lone Ranger" and "The Cisco Kid" were fantastical and childish.

As Kiet's supply of Golden Tiger dwindled, his insights increased. The similarities between himself and Marshal Dillon were notable. He and Matt towered above their contemporaries. He and Matt spoke softly and were given to reflection. His town, a frontier of sorts, and Matt's Dodge City were rife with criminal activity. Indeed, what was the essential difference between cattle rustling and Golden Peacock rustling?

That Matt carried a cannon slung low in his holster and Kiet carried no gun at all was unimportant. Nor was the frequency with which Matt demonstrated physical courage at the Longbranch Saloon and elsewhere significant. The century separating Matt's Dodge City from Kiet's Hickorn had buffered the demands for lawmen to be violent. Kiet felt that Matt's quick-draw killing of a desperado at the opening of each show was irrelevant to Hickorn, where criminals were generally sneaky. He could not visualize a pistol-shooting showdown against an opium smuggler on Avenue Dwight Eisenhower at high noon.

Sprawled on his sofa, Kiet viewed the conclusion of the second "Gunsmoke" and a phenomenon of secondary interest, an advertising message. Since no sales presentations were yet shown on Luongan television, Kiet knew that the spiel was mistakenly spliced onto the tapes.

Whatever its origins Kiet watched intently as twin

Caucasian sisters peddled chewing gum through the medium of song and dance. They had long legs, beehive hairdos, and prominent breasts. They cloyingly implored the audience to double their pleasure, double their fun.

Kiet smiled. His eyelids drooped shut. The shifty duet of Chick Chipperfield and Ambulance Al Selkirk. They would henceforth be known to him as the Doublemint Twins.

8

The dream was repetitious and black, a sing-
song "murder, murder, murder, murder" devoid of images.
Black transformed into a fireball of painful yellow. Demons
were shaking Kiet's shoulder, shaking the Earth apart.

"Superintendent, there has been a murder!"

Kiet opened his eyes and blinked. Binh's flashlight re-
sembled a monstrous firefly. He swatted at it. "A murder?"

"Superintendent, every door in your villa is unlocked. I
walked right in."

Many times since his return from America the young
captain had scolded his superior on the subject of residen-
tial security. Often he had regaled him with tales of
homicidal dope fiends breaking and entering to steal
videotape recorders and microwave ovens to finance their
habits.

"Unlocked," Kiet said, sitting up on the couch. "Murder?
Where, when? It's dark, the middle of the night."

"It is nine-thirty in the morning, Superintendent," Binh
said, yanking the living room drapes apart with peevish
gusto.

Kiet flinched at the rush of sunlight and suppressed a moan. He now empathized with vampires.

"Apparently I closed them because of glare on the television receiver," he said meekly.

The set was still on. A lean, handsome, and gregarious Caucasian in a fancy suit was playing cards, smiling and talking fast to justify the mountain of chips in front of him.

"I'm glad that you're finally taking advantage of your complimentary TV. I like 'Maverick' too," Binh said. "It's a lot of fun and James Garner is a super actor, but—"

Kiet had been craning his neck to see around his adjutant, who accidentally toppled a Golden Tiger empty with his boot as he moved aside. Binh paused, sighed dramatically, and said, "Superintendent, Alvin Selkirk was murdered last night at the National Museum."

"How?"

"I haven't been there yet. Dr. Chi reported it to uniformed officers, who reported it to Headquarters and myself. I thought it best to come for you en route. I'm told that Selkirk's skull was crushed."

"What was Selkirk doing in the National Museum?"

Binh shrugged.

"Hasn't museum security been increased, both by us and by the staff?"

"I don't think so, Superintendent. After all, the fox has already visited the hen house."

This was an Americanism Kiet understood. He excused himself to wash and dress, envying Matt Dillon, who was confronted with just one simple crime per episode.

Minister of Tourism Phorn Ridsa and two patrolmen greeted Kiet and Binh in the museum lobby. Or rather, the patrolmen did the greeting. Ridsa merely sneered.

"A veritable crime wave we have at the National Mu-

60

seum, Kiet. Is there anyone in your department who doesn't qualify for strong eyeglasses and a hearing aid?"

Shock and aspirin had cleared Kiet's head. He was in no humor to be browbeaten by this prima donna. Ridsa was tall, but Kiet had a couple of inches on him. He fixed a Dillonesque stare on the minister and asked, "When did Dr. Chi discover the body?"

"Two hours ago," Ridsa said, his eyes unmoving from Kiet's. "He's practically lived here since yesterday. He called me and your incompetent police department."

Get hold of the other Doublemint Twin, Kiet thought. He said to Binh, "I think we should speak to Mr. Chipperfield as soon as possible."

"I've sent a man on a scooter to the Continental, Superintendent."

"Where is Dr. Chi, Mr. Minister?"

"In his office, lying down," Ridsa said, his contempt undisguised. "The poor little man saw Selkirk and threw up. He isn't feeling well. You'll want to inspect the body. Come on. You'll know why I'm hurrying you when we get there."

They went into the Golden Peacock room. Ambulance Al Selkirk was face down at the foot of the vacant shrine, arms and legs extended in a skydiving configuration. Kiet began breathing through his mouth. Ridsa's insistence on haste wasn't mere impatience. At death, Selkirk had become incontinent.

"Unquestionably the murder weapon," Binh said, pointing to a melon-sized stone Buddha resting approximately a meter from Selkirk's depressed skull.

"Yes," Kiet said, happy that his attention had been diverted from the corpse. Bamsan Kiet's deepest secret was his aversion to human gore. Exposure to blood and guts flooded him with nausea. While upchucking was acceptable, even taken for granted, for a prissy intellectual like Dr. Latisa Chi, a sterner constitution was expected of

61

Hickorn's ranking police officer. If he lost the breakfast he hadn't eaten, engaging in a protracted bout of the dry heaves, Phorn Ridsa would be delighted to spread the news. By the end of the week Kiet would be professionally impotent, a notorious sissy unable to arrest a nine-year-old watch snatcher without resistance.

"See how the back of Selkirk's head is bashed in, Superintendent?" Binh said. "And the Buddha? Curly gray hairs caked onto dried blood?"

"I do," Kiet said, squinting intently, a technique that blurred his vision.

In demonstration, Binh raised his arms and flung them down. "The killer slipped behind Selkirk and clobbered him with the Buddha."

Ridsa explained, "Before the esteemed Dr. Chi retired to his sickbed, he informed me that the Buddha was carved by highlands craftsmen at the turn of the century. They made many of these artifacts to sell to the French, whose wives believed they were historic and valuable. They're crude. They cheapen the National Museum, but I applaud Chi's artistic cleverness. He displays them in hallways and at room entrances, to occupy space. Westerners associate Asia and Buddha. A museum can't have too many Buddhas. You might have noticed, Kiet, that the pedestal next to the doorway we came through has nothing on it."

"I noticed, Mr. Minister, " Kiet lied. "Thank you for your insight."

The ghoulish Binh was on his knees, groping around Selkirk and his clothing. "Whoa, what's this!"

"Excuse me?" Kiet, meanwhile, had turned his back to the grisly spectacle, feigning a clue search of the Buddha-less pedestal.

Binh sprang to his feet and gave Kiet two keys. "They were in his shirt pocket."

Kiet examined the keys. Brand names and identifying

numbers had been ground off, leaving curved grooves. "Try them," he said.

"A decent crime laboratory," Binh said wistfully. "Magnetic particle testing and X rays could bring up the characters so easily."

"We have no crime laboratory, let alone a decent one, Captain. Please try them."

Binh did. He was back in less than a minute, announcing breathlessly, "The front door and the alarm box cover. They fit. Somebody who knew the layout could have got inside within the time allotted and switched off the alarms before they sounded."

Ridsa threw up his hands. "Incredible. He walked right in, right under the noses of Hickorn's finest."

"For what purpose, please, did Mr. Selkirk walk right in under our noses?" Kiet asked Ridsa.

Ridsa shook a finger at Kiet. "If this is an accusation, you're treading in a mine field."

Kiet smiled. "Regard it as a rhetorical question if you prefer."

"They're probably duplicates," Binh said, eager to conciliate. "They could have been made from wax impressions."

"There you are, Kiet. You should listen to your young Sherlock Holmes. Chi leaves his key ring on his desk. I've chided him about that—to no avail, it seems. You've heard the stories about absentminded professors."

Kiet was unconvinced. He didn't reply.

"The business association we've had with these . . . these Americans, the trust we've placed in them," Ridsa continued. "Alvin and Chick betrayed it. They must have planned to loot National Museum from the outset."

"The onset, the birth of Unknown Asia Tours, is sketchy, Mr. Minister."

"You're making a sinister insinuation, Kiet. I'd advise you to remember whom you're talking to. The arrangement was pragmatic and aboveboard. We wished to increase tourism and a concomitant increase in hard currency. The Chipperfield-Selkirk proposal was the most lucrative for Luong."

"Cheeseburgers and television," Kiet muttered.

"Those were incentives to us. Luong has a primitive image in the West and—"

"I understand your rationale," Kiet interrupted. "Tourists must be enticed with guarantees that they will not be housed in jungle huts."

"Exactly," Ridsa said. "A comfort zone."

"Splendid. We cannot live without our zones. Please elaborate on the negotiations. Who and when."

Phorn Ridsa shook his head. "Sorry, Kiet. Negotiations are confidential. And irrelevant."

"Irrelevant? An Unknown Asia Tours partner is dead, murdered. The Golden Peacock is missing. Any background you can provide, I think, is exceedingly relevant."

"I disagree. We were cheated and misled by confidence men. We were victims of a plot to steal our treasures. I accept blame for trusting them. I've lost face and I'll probably lose my job too. The past is the past. We should be concentrating on the future, Kiet, on cutting our losses. Recovering the Golden Peacock and arresting Chick Chipperfield for the murder of Alvin Selkirk are the priorities."

Ridsa spoke too lackadaisically to suit Kiet. They were not the anxious words of a man suffering a shattering loss of face. They were calm and calculated words of persuasion, words meant to manipulate the investigation. Kiet said, "You were victimized by a victim of the ultimate crime, Mr. Minister."

"Don't ask me to mourn the bastard," Ridsa said evenly.

Kiet groaned. "Sir, I'm not asking for grief. I'm asking for facts and logic. The Golden Peacock was stolen the *night before last*. What was Mr. Selkirk doing here *last night* being bludgeoned with a Buddha?"

64

"How often do I have to repeat myself, Kiet? Chipper-field."

"You said who, Mr. Minister. You are not saying why."

"Why what?"

Kiet gritted his teeth. He did not give a damn that his grimace was unsuitable. He spoke slowly, as if instructing a child who could not fathom long division. "Why did Mr. Selkirk and Mr. Chipperfield, Mr. Selkirk's alleged killer, return to National Museum last night? Presumably the Golden Peacock was in their possession. What was to be gained by risking a second burglary? Silk panels and gilded statues are precious in their own right, but infinitesimal in value compared to the Peacock."

Phorn Ridsa sighed, raised his eyebrows, and shook his head—a theatrical triad. He said, "Westerners are inscrutable, you know."

"Twice in two days I've heard *inscrutable*. This pair isn't stupid. Wasn't stupid."

Ridsa said, "Immeasurable greed defies discretion."

"A splendid cliché, Mr. Minister. You are claiming, then, that Chipperfield and Selkirk came for more loot and had a falling out? Or Chipperfield desired it all?"

"I claim nothing, Kiet. You're the detective. I'm only trying to guide you toward the obvious."

"A path I shall gratefully follow, Mr. Minister," Kiet said, turning, nodding for Binh to follow.

"Chipperfield," Ridsa reminded. "In retrospect, I should've known that any man who dresses so grotesquely is capable of many things, but—"

"But you are not a detective, sir. Thank you again. We will find him soon, I assure you."

In the lobby, Binh said, "What about the stiff?"

"Pardon me?"

Binh wrinkled his nose. "The body."

"Fresh air," Kiet said, inhaling deeply. "Wonderful stuff.

National Museum is not equipped with an icebox. Have it removed."

"No secrecy, Superintendent?"

"Secrecy regarding a murder isn't feasible, especially the murder of a foreign national. Our Golden Peacock secret is of greater importance and it is relatively safe."

"You feel that we can count on Dr. Chi?"

"Absolutely. After his tummy quiets, he will stand guard at our barricade of lies."

"We aren't going to question him now, are we, Superintendent?"

"No."

Kiet's adjutant grinned. "We will later, though, in *our* element, not while he's under Minister Ridsa's thumb?"

"Sometimes we link telepathically, Captain. We will indeed. Ridsa's dominance of the absentminded professor is—"

"Utterly and overwhelmingly counterproductive to a breakthrough stroking session."

At least a major impediment, Kiet thought, wondering if there was any room in true telepathy for so many adjectives. "Yes."

A department motor scooter arrived, exhaust popping, belching blue smoke. The driver beeped its pathetic horn. Binh ran outside. The officer snapped a smart salute. Binh returned it with equal crispness, conferred, and rejoined Kiet.

"The man you sent for Chipperfield?"

"Yeah. Chipperfield wasn't at the Continental. My man nosed around and traced him down. Would you like to guess where?"

Binh's voice was an octave higher than normal. "No," Kiet said. "No, I would not like to guess. Where, please?"

"The United States embassy. He's applying for political asylum."

66

9

"Mr. Chipperfield is gone, Mr. Ambassador?"

"We had no grounds to detain him, Superintendent Kiet," said Ambassador Smithson. "Conversely, we had no justification for allowing him to remain on the premises under his own volition. The poor fellow was confused and agitated. With considerable difficulty, we stated official policy to Mr. Chipperfield. Requests for political asylum are processed only for citizens of the host nation. Fortunately, no asylum applications have been made in my tenure. Knock on wood. They open a real can of worms, you know. A parallel, however absurd, would be a Luongan national applying to the Luongan embassy in Washington."

Absurd? Bamsan Kiet had never traveled outside Luong's borders and never intended to. The mad and violent pace of North America and Western Europe was a matter of record. So what was absurd about a panicked dash to tranquility?

Kiet was on the fourth and top floor of the year-old

United States embassy building, a steel and glass box dubbed the Glass Palace by cynics, himself included. Air conditioning was permanently set on subarctic. Invisible speakers dispensed violin music in offices and the elevator. Fuzzy carpeting *everywhere*, tropically lush and taller than the treads of his sandals, functioned as a static electricity dynamo; he couldn't touch anything without receiving a fingertip sting. Sophisticated acoustics banished all noise except the *thunk-thunk* of computer keyboards. The place was, in a word, peculiar.

"Did Mr. Chipperfield give a reason for his request, sir?"

Ambassador Smithson frowned thoughtfully before replying. He was lean and fiftyish, gray-maned and immaculately attired in three-piece pinstripes, a member of a Western power clique known as Ivy League Eastern Establishment. "He did. He was holding back on me, I'm certain, but he seemed to fear political opposition to Unknown Asia Tours and the kudos its success has afforded Prince Pakse's regime."

"Specifically, please?"

"The assassination of his partner and himself by a professional hit team."

"Assassination?"

"I know, his phraseology was a tad flatulent. The fellow is a flamboyant dresser and a mile-a-minute jabberer, but we were able to sift through the slang and crudities to assess his concern as marginally viable. Accordingly, I relayed the information to you."

Speaking of flatulent, Kiet thought. He asked, "Assassinated by whom, please?"

Ambassador Smithson winked grimly. "If we are to accept his frantic assertion, it's as plain as the noses on our faces, I'd say."

Oh no, Kiet thought, here we go again. Yesterday, a primer on imperialist terrorism from Ambassador Dang. Today, the opposite view. Communism obsessed Smithson

68

and the past American president who appointed him to Hickorn. They believed in the Domino Theory with religious fervor. Laos, Cambodia, and Vietnam had fallen a decade and a half ago. The fourth Indochinese domino, the Luongan, remained cemented in bedrock, but these were men of faith. If Asian reds could not topple it, perhaps a nudge from afar, from Nicaragua or wherever, would do the trick. Or, as Smithson would soon sermonize, there might be an attempt to uproot by the local Marxist variety.

Smithson went on, "The Rouge have been quiet lately, haven't they?"

"Yes," Kiet agreed, thinking that the Luong Rouge were usually quiet. They had no choice. The Rouge movement began in the early 1960s and had accomplished little, stagnated by a chronic shortage of money and supplies.

Rouge leaders refused all overtures of outside aid. A revolution was not a revolution if Russians and Chinese and North Koreans and Vietnamese walked Hickorn's streets bearing checkbooks and wonderful advice. The Rouge bided their time in the highlands, scruffy guerrilla bands that occasionally ambushed a truck convoy and mortared an army barracks.

With incredible patience they waited for an internal eruption. Kiet could not resist admiring Rouge idealism, but wondered if they had been in the hills too long, subsisting on inadequate diets. Workers and peasants had no shackles to throw off. His Royal Highness taxed farmers equitably. They ate their fill of the crops they grew and sold the surplus, unburdened by unfair levies. Urban dwellers also lived freely. Monarchal oppression was a morose fantasy.

Ambassador Smithson stroked his jaw thoughtfully and said, "Suppose, Superintendent Kiet, just suppose, that Chipperfield has gotten wind of something?"

"Something, Mr. Ambassador?"

"A plot. Even a bare inkling of a plot, mind you."

"A plot?"

"A conspiracy. Nobody can deny that tourism has been a marvelous boon to Luong's economy."

"Nobody," Kiet said.

"Tourism may eventually become Luong's industrial base, as it were."

"Eventually," Kiet said.

"What discourages tourism?"

"Amoebic dysentery?"

Smithson laughed. "Excellent. But no. I'm alluding to a stronger deterrent. Danger!"

"Danger to the tourists?"

"Indirectly. If the architects of Unknown Asia Tours are in mortal danger, can the average traveler feel safe in Luong? No, of course he can't. If one strives to dry up the trade, what better timing than at Savhanakip? Who, I ask, stands to gain from the resulting turmoil and political embarrassment?"

Kiet was expected to contribute and reluctantly did. "The Rouge?"

"Exactly! And television multiplies the incentive."

Ah, television. Kiet closed his eyes and rewarded himself with a flashback of Matt Dillon's powerful fists, weapons of vengeance applied to a cowardly criminal who menaced Doc Adams at the Longbranch. He said, "'Gunsmoke.'"

Smithson smiled indulgently. "Oh, I'll grant you that the anachronistic horse operas on Channel Seven possess a modicum of entertainment value, but they only scratch the surface. The vast potential of Luongan television is yet to be realized. The Rouge understand that potential."

Anachronistic horse operas? Kiet flushed. "They do?"

"I've jawboned Minister of Tourism Ridsa on the subject, Superintendent Kiet. He agrees in principle with me that the medium can and must be elevated to a higher plane. The pragmatic philosophy of entertaining and pacifying visitors is a stepping stone to long-term goals, and Minister

Ridsa is a forward thinker. I envision in the not-too-distant future a release of prime-time segments to news and public information programming. The latter is especially exciting and I've pledged to cover funding shortfalls."

Public information programming? Kiet translated: propaganda. "Splendid, sir," he said without enthusiasm.

"In a way, it's a pity you're so valuable in your chosen profession. You'd make a great anchorman. You're a large man and you're respected. You have charisma. You'd be a natural on the small screen."

Kiet deduced from Smithson's sincere smile and effusive hand gestures that he had been paid a high compliment, but Captain Binh's descriptions of American anchormen and anchorwomen, while also laudatory, made him wonder. Binh's praise of their hair and white teeth and flawless diction conjured in Kiet's mind mannequins hollowed out and furnished with tape recorders. "Uh, thank you, sir."

"Am I out of line for smelling a rat?"

Kiet took a notebook out of his pocket and busily scribbled notes, a sign to the ambassador that immediate action would be forthcoming, a sign that would hopefully change the topic of conversation. "No, sir. On the contrary, you have enlightened me."

"Don't forget, Superintendent Kiet, rats congregate. They're voracious and social."

Kiet knew what was coming but didn't want to listen to it. He scribbled faster, as if the insinuation alone were sufficient. It wasn't.

Smithson asked, "How long have the Vietnamese been in Hickorn? Approximately?"

"Not long. Six, seven, perhaps eight months."

"*Too* long. That is how long, Superintendent Kiet. Soviet chicanery in Luong is legend, but beware the Vietnamese. They could teach their masters a trick or two. That porcine little Dang, that degenerate—watch him like a hawk! Dang is capable of forging a Rouge-Vietnamese axis if anyone is."

Kiet could never tell whether Americans had the capacity to lose face as devastatingly as did Luongans. Their emotions were so elastic. Land a setback or a humiliation on a Yankee and he would counterpunch with a hard smile and a quip.

Kiet looked at Smithson. The utterance, the reference to the hated Vietnamese, the upcoming Luong-Vietnam soccer match, the vile memory of the Avenue Vo Nguyen Giap redesignation—all this had discredited him. Possibly he had not lost face, but color was emptying from it.

"Establishment of diplomatic relations with Vietnam was sensible," Kiet said. "Laos borders us and Laos is a Vietnamese client. If you hang out your laundry on the same fence, you should smile back and forth."

"A witty analogy," Smithson said coldly. "Never mind that your smiling neighbor is ready, willing, and able to steal your underwear."

Enough, Kiet thought. Fifteen minutes in the ambassadorial chambers, shivering in the air conditioning, enduring political word games. Enough. He related the murder of Ambulance Al Selkirk.

"Good gravy!" Smithson exclaimed. "In the National Museum?"

"Regrettably so. Mr. Chipperfield came to you fearing assassination. Was his fear expressed in the past tense?"

"Did he know? I—I don't think so, but such knowledge could explain his frenzied state."

"It could," Kiet agreed.

"Do you suspect him?"

"I am anxious to speak to him, sir."

"If I had only known, I'd've delayed him. What tangled webs we weave, eh? I'd crossed paths with Selkirk on occasion. He seemed a decent sort. An attorney, as I recall."

A disbarred attorney, Kiet knew. "Yes."

"I practiced the profession," Smithson said reflectively. "Yale undergrad, Harvard Law, Wall Street. A useful ap-

72

prenticeship for statecraft, some might say. You will keep me up to speed as the case develops, Superintendent Kiet?"

"Yes, sir."

"Bear in mind that the idol may be troublesome somewhere down the road."

The idol? The Golden Peacock? Kiet conceded with dismay that the rumor had reached this icy tower. Still, give the man nothing. "The idol, sir?"

"The making of a headache. Mark my words."

Not a problem, Kiet thought nastily: no brain, no headache. "Pardon me?"

"The Buddha. The killer clobbered Selkirk with a religious object, you said. A Buddha. That's a sacrilege any way you slice it. We don't want any feathers ruffled this close to Savhanakip. I'm not a detective, Superintendent Kiet, but I'd strongly recommend that the murder weapon be kept confidential. Selective confidentiality, as it were."

Kiet smiled in relief. Smithson had not heard the Golden Peacock story and he would not hear it now. Kiet stood and shook hands. The static-electrical discharge between their fingers was a painless tingle. "Thank you, Mr. Ambassador. Selective confidentiality is a splendid recommendation."

O n   h i s   drive to Headquarters, Kiet passed the Postal Office. It was a substantial stone building with Doric columns, an edifice that suggested solidity and service to the public. A deceptive appearance if you asked Lin Aidit or almost anybody else, Kiet thought.

He saw Quoc, the leprous beggar with no nose, squatting on the entrance steps. Kiet was pleased that Quoc had complied and removed himself and his alms cup from Luong Burgers and its complaining manager.

Quoc spotted Kiet. He grinned and waved.

"The airport too," Kiet shouted out the car window.

"Tourists boarding airplanes may have a few zin in their pockets they can never spend."

Quoc's grin broadened. He nodded and fanned skeletal arms. Kiet saluted and continued on, his mood lifted by the pariah's obvious adoration. A satisfied police customer. There were so few.

10

''No,'' Binh said in answer to Kiet's question. "No progress whatsoever on the Golden Peacock. Zilch. It hasn't gone through Hickorn International, though. I'd stake my life on it, Superintendent."

"Your inquiries in town?"

"Since they must be discreet and made by myself and a handful of trusted officers, no results either. We can't probe too hard. We'd be authenticating the rumor. I can't count the number of people who have dropped in or telephoned, asking if it's true. I hate lying, Superintendent. I've told more lies in two days than I normally do in an entire year."

Kiet nodded sadly. They were in his office, Kiet at his desk, Binh across from him. Binh was doodling on a notepad. Kiet could not imagine blank note paper and this sort of hapless inaction in the Dodge City marshal's office. "Developments on the Selkirk murder investigation?"

Binh shook his head. "The same. Zip. Chipperfield is our critical lead there, but he vanished after he left the Glass Palace. Him and his land yacht."

"Land yacht? He owns an amphibious boat?"

"No. Chipperfield's 1962 Chrysler, Superintendent. That's what they call those massive old cars. Twenty and thirty years ago, you couldn't sell a car in the United States unless it had tail fins and chrome from end to end. Nowadays, Americans buy Toyotas, except in Detroit—"

"All right!" Kiet said, breaking off Binh's folklore lesson. "We are suffocating in negatives. We need positives."

"A goal-oriented investigative approach is essential," Binh said, absently drawing sharp arrows on his pad.

"Whatever," Kiet said. "Until we apprehend Mr. Chipperfield, Dr. Latisa Chi strikes me as the soft spot."

Binh smiled. "Likewise. When can we bring him in? My overhauled polygraph awaits."

"We should not attach wires to the distinguished curator, Captain, until we have a list of distressing questions to ask."

"Yeah, leverage," Binh said. "We're running a background check on him."

"And?"

"He's a real dull guy, Superintendent. A bachelor. Frugal life-style. He's in the National Museum twelve hours a day, reading and dusting exhibits."

"I wonder if an unconventional check would be useful."

"What do you mean?"

"Lin Aidit, the tour guide, is a friend of yours, is she not?"

Binh's expression relaxed. A carnal memory? "I've taken her to the cinema. Lin is a groovy date."

"She told me that Channel Seven is Channel Seven because Dr. Chi deems seven a lucky number."

"Gambling?"

"To throw a seven is a dice player's heaven, is it not?"

Binh sketched a quartering view of a die, replete with dots. "Sure is. Maybe he has a secret life. Maybe he's got problems. I'll dig in that direction."

There was a knock on the door. Binh scowled and said, "I gave instructions that we were in conference."

"What else can we accomplish? Come in."

Madame Mai Le Trung, Vietnamese cultural attaché and designated soccer liaison, entered and said to Kiet, "I apologize for the intrusion, Superintendent. I earlier attempted to contact you for an appointment, but your desk personnel said you were in the field working on cases. I took a chance that I might find you in."

No genuflection this time, Kiet noticed. But her smile was winning and respectful, a more than adequate compensation. He introduced Madame Mai to Captain Binh, who released his hand long before he released his eyes. His gaze was a fusion of lust and contempt. He was a virile young man with minimal tolerance for communists, whether they came with nice breasts or not.

"That matter we were discussing, Captain?"

"Right away, Superintendent. Will do," Binh said, taking the hint and his leave.

"You wish to verify security for your soccer team, Madame?" Kiet asked, gesturing to Binh's vacated chair.

She sat and said, "I would, providing you have an hour or two to spare."

"Of course." Her silken *áo dài* was loose fitting and layered over equally loose-fitting pants and blouse. It was not an erotic garment. So why was it?

"I thank you. Is it true that an American businessman was murdered in your National Museum?"

"True."

"Thus the time I request is precious to you," she said, speaking faster. "The team is to be billeted at our embassy. Our guards will protect them while there. Their arrival at the airport and safe passage to the embassy, I feel, is our joint responsibility."

"Agreed."

"The game at National Stadium too?"

"Yes."

"Those situations are relatively static. Post your men

77

properly and the perils of each can be anticipated in advance."

"They shall be, Madame," Kiet said. "Or should I be calling you Comrade? Ambassador Dang addressed you as Madame, but I do not want to be improper."

"Madame Mai is better. Mai is best. Comrade is too stiff and stilted. Don't tell anybody I said that or I'll be branded a reactionary," she said, laughing. "And, yes, I do accept your security assurances. Ambassador Dang has supreme respect for you."

"Thank you," Kiet said cautiously, remembering Dang's serpentine logic.

"Please don't be insulted, Superintendent, but Ambassador Dang and I do worry about the Savhanakip parade, in which the team is obligated to participate. The route is five kilometers long."

"Four-point-eight kilometers," Kiet said, trying to demonstrate a grasp of details. In fact, he was depressingly reminded, the Golden Peacock and Selkirk diversions had prevented finalization of Savhanakip details. Scores of them.

"Through teeming city streets, thousands of spectators an arm's length from the paraders," Mai continued.

"I intend to assign rovers, Madame Mai, plainclothesmen on the lookout for strange behavior. Of course, even if I had a division of soldiers at my disposal—two divisions, ten divisions—prevention of a tragedy is impossible."

"I know," she said, sighing. "World history is stained by the acts of one man, one weapon."

"Would a drive along the parade route ease your anxieties?"

Madame Mai said yes, thank you, and sprang out of her chair. It has happened to me again, Kiet realized. These Vietnamese. Yesterday Dan, today Mai. Engineering their will through the back door of mine.

78

"We can go immediately if it is convenient," he said needlessly.

'' T h e Savhanakip parade begins there, " Kiet said. He had parked his Citroën on Mu Savhana, at the National Bank. They were facing the Royal Palace, two blocks to the south. Mu Savhana ended at the palace's gates. Cement and ornamental iron sealed lush emerald grounds and the mansion of white stone centered thereon. Critics, especially fuzzy-headed academics and nationalistic zealots, ridiculed the baroque French architecture. A pre-Independence ghost, they whined; a neocolonial mockery. To hell with them, Kiet thought. The Royal Palace and the man who inhabited it were national treasures.

"Beautifully decadent," Madame Mai said.

An odd pairing of words. Was this communist humor? Kiet said, "The Royal party assembles at the gates. Elephant farms near Hickorn train their animals to harvest timber. The brightest and most docile student is chosen and delivered the night before. It is a great honor for the trainer, so the farms always set aside several elephants that learn nothing but how to carry a human being on pavement without jolting his kidneys loose.

"Prince Pakse mounts the elephant litter and proceeds. Luongan dignitaries and distinguished foreign guests, including the Luongan and Vietnamese soccer squads, follow in automobiles."

Kiet swept an arm northward to the National Museum, which was just beyond Avenue Irving Crane, the next cross street. He continued: "The caravan stops at the National Museum. A ministry chief receives the Golden Peacock from the curator, climbs a ladder, and places it on His Royal Highness' head. Our ministers take turns. This year is the Minister of Agriculture's."

79

"I've gone to the National Museum," Mai said. "Your Golden Peacock is a fabulous work of art."

Not for an instant during his monologue had Kiet's eyes moved from the Vietnamese woman's. He had been watching for a flicker, a reaction to anything he had said, an involuntary betrayal. He had no solid cause to believe that the Vietnamese and this woman were in any way culpable in recent events, nor could he speculate on entwinement in future shenanigans, but he had no reason not to be suspicious either. He discerned nothing from her, even at his reference to the National Museum and her mention of the Golden Peacock. Nothing. Binh's zip and zilch.

They got into the car and began tracing the parade route. Kiet decided not to narrate. If Mai had questions, let her ask. She leaned forward in her seat, scanning left and right. Kiet inhaled for the first time a floral scent. He wondered if she wore perfume in Hanoi, if such a wonderful toiletry would be regarded as counterrevolutionary.

They turned left onto Mu Hickorn. There were many cinemas and open-air cafés along the bustling street. Odors of fish, meats, and sauces wafted through the Citroën, temporarily overpowering Madame Mai's enticing aroma. Cinema marquees were postered and hand painted. Chinese and Indian films seemed to be featured this week. Those fierce and dreadful kung fu epics out of Hong Kong and Taiwan. Maudlin Hindu romances, fragile heroines draped in saris, their faces peculiarly dotted with paint. Ah, there on one poster, Sabu the jungle boy. An old, old film; a classic. Kiet liked Sabu. After Savhanakip, he would attend.

Left onto Rue Ho Chi Minh. The cathedral and City Hall, now known as Hickorn Center for Public Administration. Crossing Avenue Dwight Eisenhower, also known as Le Avenue, a thoroughfare of chic shops that catered to foreigners and rich Luongans.

"Tu Do," Mai said, looking back as they went through the intersection.

"Excuse me?"

"Your Le Avenue is like Tu Do Street in Ho Chi Minh City. During the French occupation it was Rue Catinat. No difference. Every oppressed and underdeveloped nation has a Le Avenue, a Tu Do, where the spoils of greed and corruption are spent."

"Le Avenue's shoppers have money and I cannot dispute greed and corruption. Does Tu Do still exist in—" Kiet almost slipped and said Saigon, a serious gaffe to these Vietnamese communists. "—Ho Chi Minh City?"

"Not as blatantly as before Liberation. The cockroach is reputed to be an indestructible species. Black marketeers survive well too."

Kiet did not pursue the subject. Madame Mai was obviously sensitive to it and he wasn't entirely certain whether her scorn was inspired by politics or envy. The Vietnamese dong was sicklier than the sickly Luongan zin. The stipend she received for her embassy duties was presumably small and utterly worthless to Le Avenue's merchants. If she coveted a brooch or a stylish haircut or a leather handbag, she could only dream.

Right turn on Avenue Ronald Reagan. A park. Offices. A bar. A machine shop. A warehouse. Two blocks and another right onto Ma San Boulevard, which curved northward, paralleling the river.

"Docks," Kiet said, cocking a thumb, tired of the silence.

Madame Mai leaned toward Kiet, peering between him and the steering wheel. A silk sleeve touched his bare forearm. Her perfumed fragrance intensified, blending with her breath.

"I see only fishing boats and grain barges," she said.

"Primarily. Hickorn is no port for freighters and battle-ships. Luong is landlocked. Rice is grown up and down the Ma San, close by the water source. Paddy is sacked and milled at Hickorn. My sister and her husband are farmers, twenty kilometers upriver."

"And why don't you also farm, Superintendent?"

Kiet shook his head. "I help out at planting, but I do not enjoy a sore back and moldy feet."

Mai's laugh was musical. She touched his arm and said, "National Stadium. Why was it built on an island?"

Kiet felt a shiver. He said, "The space was sufficient, unused, and convenient. Hickorn residents can walk or bicycle there if they cannot afford a pedicab or a taxi ride. The alternative would have been to hack down jungle kilometers from town."

Kiet drove onto the Foh Ten Bridge. Concrete-and-steel trusses joined Hickorn and the horrific slum of the same name. Tin-and-scrap wood shacks on the other side of the river were home to Luong's destitute and to fugitives from both the law and personal responsibility. He half expected an acid comment on Foh Ten, on capitalistic inequities, but none was made.

The Foh Ten Bridge was actually two short bridges spanning the river on either side of the narrow tip of Savhana Island. This design was easier for the French civil engineers who constructed the arches. Kiet exited the east channel span and swung left to the stadium access road. He parked in a lot empty but for maintenance trucks, a bus, and two department motorbikes.

"I post men around the clock prior to Savhanakip, Madame," Kiet said. "At game time, I trust there will be no *plastique* affixed to the undersides of bleachers."

"Excellent," Mai said. "Can we go in?"

"Come."

National Stadium was an unpretentious oval of iron framework supporting flat wooden benches. A small chained-off section of padded theater chairs at midfield was reserved for important persons, notably Prince Pakse and his entourage. Aside from that, forty thousand seats were democratically uncomfortable.

Maintenance men worked at the near end, replacing divots of sod, manicuring grass with hand shears, and laying chalk lines. The Luongan team was practicing passes and shots at the far goal. Kiet's officers were sitting on the team bench, smoking cigarettes, not necessarily scouting for the deployment of plastic explosives. They spotted their superintendent, jumped up, and saluted. Kiet forgave their boredom and waved.

The squad ran a play. A winger sailed his service ball high over the goal mouth. The opposite winger chased it to the sideline and booted a weak roller to the target man, who volleyed wide. A crimson-faced trainer blew his whistle. A second cupped his eyes.

Kiet groaned and muttered to himself, "How many goals will we lose by this year?"

Madame Mai, apparently not a football aficionada, was studying the Royal section. "After the game, what is the itinerary for the honored guests and the teams? Is there a reverse parade?"

"No. Dignitaries are returned to town in military vehicles. By the completion of the game, much alcohol will have been consumed here and in Hickorn. Emotions are volatile, particularly in the event Luong is defeated."

"I am impressed," Mai said. "I will report to Ambassador Dang that you are doing all that can be done."

"Thank you."

"I have a final and insignificant worry. Our team arrives at the airport the day after tomorrow. May we . . . ?"

We may indeed, Kiet said. He chauffeured her to Hickorn International. The terminal was a shabby, stucco affair. Foreign visitors accustomed to the congested lunacy at New York and Tokyo airfields routinely expressed amazement that something so seedy and sleepy could be the main terminus of and the gateway to a capital city.

Kiet, an accused foe of progress, was not insulted, least of all now. The languor was a blessing. How much simpler it would be for one to smuggle a certain gold and bejeweled object out of the Kingdom of Luong if one was a proverbial sardine in an overpacked tin of travelers.

No flights were at present landing or taking off. Despite the tourism influx, there were lulls. No stopover passengers were dozing at benches or berating uninterested ticket agents because their luggage had defected at Delhi or Jakarta. Madame Mai counted thirty-one people. Kiet informed here that five of the thirty-one were not civilians.

"Plainclothes policemen?" she whispered.

Kiet nodded smugly.

"I *am* impressed," she said. "Your people are in position to protect our soccer team two days in advance?"

"Yes. I believe in anticipating any contingency," Kiet lied. The five men, of course, were Captain Binh's, officers charged with preventing the Golden Peacock's departure.

"I'm satisfied," she said. "I am done intruding in your busy day."

"Permit me to buy you a refreshment before we leave," Kiet said.

"You've been so kind. You don't have to."

"A purely selfish motive, Madame," he said, escorting her to the cocktail lounge. "My throat is parched."

They took a table at windows that overlooked the runways. Kiet ordered a Golden Tiger, Mai a bottle of mineral water. Was this the preferred libation of ascetic guerrilla fighters? He did not ask. He did not speak at all, nor did Mai. They were content to slip from their cold, perspiring bottles in the spongy lounge chairs, resting and gazing outside.

An airliner landed and taxied in. It was a plump twin-engined Boeing jet, the thrice-weekly Bangkok shuttle. Ground crewmen pushed a wheeled ladder to its door. Approximately fifty passengers disembarked.

Some were Luongan, some Thai. Over half were American and Japanese, their eyes blinking, their necks craning. A fresh consignment of Unknown Asia Tour customers. Kiet recognized nobody initially, although one man, a chubby Luongan, tickled his memory cells.

Minutes later, too late for any action, memory cells finally responded. As if undressing a child's doll, Kiet mentally stripped away the blue business suit, the white shirt, and the navy tie. He replaced the staid clothing with a garish outfit Binh had described as an obsolete American fashion entitled Polyester Leisure Suit. He added a clunky gold necklace. He shaved the goatee and discarded the glasses.

The man was Minister of Tourism Phorn Ridsa's crony, whom Kiet had exiled a year ago. Fop Tia, ex-Mayor of Hickorn, had returned to Luong incognito.

Kiet gulped his Golden Tiger too fast and had a coughing fit. When he recovered, Mai asked, "Did your beer go down wrong?"

"In a sense, Madame," Kiet rasped. "Wrong. Yes. Definitely."

11

Kiet dropped Mai off at the Vietnamese embassy and spent the afternoon at Headquarters catching up on paperwork. He despised this aspect of police work, this drudgery of reports, petty policymaking, and interdepartmental memoranda. Frustration made the bureaucratic housekeeping doubly tedious. He was not resolving the Golden Peacock and Ambulance Al Selkirk messes by signing his name to documents and writing numbers on printed forms. Consequently, he experienced no guilt when he headed home early.

He timed his departure precisely. He estimated how long it would take to put himself in his living room, situated on his sofa, just as theme music played and credits of the first of two "Gunsmoke" episodes filled the black-and-white television screen.

Kiet climbed out of the Citroën, released the latch to his gate, and saw an obstacle to his plans. He walked onto his property and then to the obstruction that had been somehow shoehorned into his tiny courtyard. He marveled at how competently the custard and silver automotive colossus had been backed in without sustaining damage. The pathway between gleaming sheet metal and masonry walls was so narrow that he would have had to travel its length sideways.

Admiration of motoring ability yielded to anger. Kiet looked at the 1962 Chrysler's four chromium headlamp pods and wished he were wearing boots rather than sandals. He would have kicked them out. He kicked in the front door of his villa instead. It was already ajar, so his anger was manifested painlessly.

"Hi, guy."

Chick Chipperfield spoke from the sofa. His shoeless, white-stockinged feet were propped on an ottoman. Kiet's nameless cat was sleeping abnormally heavily on his lap, its head resting on the Golden Tiger nestled in Chipperfield's crotch. The television was blaring.

"My adjutant nags me for not locking my doors," Kiet said, brushing by Chipperfield to reduce the volume and to adjust the antenna. "Perhaps I should listen to him."

"Lucky for me. I'll tell you, I was between a rock and a hard place. After those dildos at the U. S. of A. embassy gave me the runaround, I didn't know whether to shit or go blind."

A medical abnormality that combined intestinal and ocular malfunctions? In Chipperfield's case, a biological impossibility that might well have been possible. Kiet flicked a fingernail against the antenna mast and eliminated Miss Kitty's lovely shadow. He said, "You could have surrendered at Headquarters."

"Surrender, hell! I haven't done a damn thing. I'm here for *protection*. If I go to your police station and you aren't there to explain things to, your gendarmes'd toss me in the slammer and throw away the key."

Kiet looked at the tourism entrepreneur, the former automobile merchant, the surviving Doublemint Twin. He stared beyond Chick Chipperfield's blustering facade, into his eyes. He saw terror. "You requested political asylum. You told Ambassador Smithson you feared assassination by professional hitsters."

Chipperfield nodded eagerly. "Yeah, hit men. Commies is how I clock it."

Kiet said, "Because Unknown Asia Tours' success improves Luong's economy and undermines the Rouge's propaganda campaign, which is based primarily on dissatisfaction?"

"Yeah, right on the button. Smithson, he's a stuffed shirt but he's no dummy. That's the way he's got it doped out too. He knows the score."

Kiet noticed a saucer of Golden Tiger on the floor beside Chipperfield's end of the sofa. The comatose cat shared its master's weakness for the brew. "Indeed? Has there been an attempt on your life?"

"Well, no, but when you been around like I have you feel vibrations. You know the other shoe's about to drop."

"Is your partner, Mr. Selkirk, also worried?"

"Yeah, sure. He's no fool."

"Where is he now, please?"

Chipperfield took a long swallow. Air bubbles rushed up inside the bottle. He patted his stomach, belched softly, and said, "That stuff's not really too shabby. Your cat doesn't mind it either. I owe you."

"You did not answer my question."

"Don't bullshit a bullshitter, Kiet. Al's dead and I'm going apeshit cuz he is. I'm next on the hit list."

"He *is* no fool, you said. Present tense. You are being as coy with me as you were at your embassy."

"Okay, okay. I knew."

"When did you learn of Mr. Selkirk's death?"

"I got a phone call at my hotel room. Woke me out of a sound sleep."

"From whom?"

"Latisa Chi."

"From the National Museum?"

"Yeah. Poor little nerd. I could hardly make out what he was saying. He'd just got done puking his guts out."

"What, please, was Mr. Selkirk doing at the National Museum in the middle of the night?"

"Hey, how should I know? Al was free, white, and twenty-one. He was a big boy."

"Did the big boy ever confide in you how he happened to possess a museum key?"

"A key. No. Uh-uh. That's new to me."

"I am perfectly willing, Mr. Chipperfield, to provide you protection."

Chipperfield clapped his hands, then rubbed them together. "I knew I was on the beam coming to your house, Kiet. I heard you was A-OK. Gimme twenty-four hours to settle up my affairs, make airline reservations, and I'll be outta here. I'll run Unknown Asia Tours by remote control from Bangkok. Life's too short for this political assassination jazz."

"Protection in exchange for information."

"I gave you all I know," he said, his eyes wide with innocence.

Chester had just burst into the Marshal's office, trailing his bum leg, babbling to Matt about a fast-gun stranger who was "pickin' on" folks at the Longbranch. Kiet groaned; he would miss some splendid early action. He grabbed Chipperfield by a wrist and wrenched him to his feet. Kiet's cat somersaulted, landed on all fours, hissed, and scuttled into the kitchen.

"Hey!" Chipperfield dug in his white-stockinged heels at the door. "Where we going?"

"*You*, sir, are going. Your destination is of no interest to me."

"You're killing me, Kiet, sure as you're sticking a gun down my throat."

Kiet had him outside, backpedaling. He slammed him against the Chrysler and said, "Information."

Chipperfield refused eye contact and said, "Could be I sort of missed a tidbit or two, but you gotta believe that I'm being fairly honest with you, all things considered."

"*Fairly* honest?"

"Okay, fine," Chipperfield said. "You got me by the shorts. If I'm not mistaken, there's more of those Golden Tigers in your icebox, right?"

"Come," Kiet said.

T h e y didn't speak until the first "Gunsmoke" concluded. The fast-gun stranger raising havoc in the Longbranch turned out to be the kid brother of another fast-gun Matt had outdrawn. He had ridden into Dodge City seeking vengeance. Matt sent him on his way, a wiser and less malevolent man. Reason had triumphed over violence. Kiet was touched.

"Whom, please, did Mr. Selkirk say he was meeting last night?"

"Phorn Ridsa."

"Why?"

"Al didn't say. He just told me that Ridsa needed to see him on urgent business. Al, my ol' *kemo sabey*, God rest his soul, probably figured he'd clue me in later. I'd just be guessing."

"Guess," Kiet said.

"Your numero uno trinket, which you were feeling us out about yesterday on the *terrasse*. The shiny headgear. It's no secret somebody ripped it off the night before. This town of yours, Kiet, if you could bottle gossip and sell it for five bucks a jug, you'd be a millionaire. Ridsa's been jumping through hoops. If Al had a key like you claim, well, maybe Ridsa pegged him as the thief."

"A correct presumption?"

91

"Nah. Me and Al, we were married to sisters and we were partners, yeah, but I never one hundred percent trusted him. I wouldn't've put it past him, but I'd've known."

"Describe your alliance with Minister Ridsa."

Chipperfield smirked. "Mr. Personality. Guy has a Hitler complex. He loves power. UAT was his baby and we'd damn well better dance to his music or else. I think he gets his jollies bossing white men around. Me and Al, we were making money, so what the hell. UAT and Luong Burgers are going great guns. Once we got on track selling commercials, TV'd be a gold mine too. We played Ridsa's game, called him sir and kissed his fanny, the whole thing."

"The genesis of Unknown Asia Tours remains cloudy."

"That's a question? Okay. Me and Al, we'd split the sheets with our old ladies. They were in the travel business, so we'd traveled some on the cheap. We liked the Far East. It's kind of wide open and broads know their place, unlike those barracudas we were married to, but that's another story. Anyway, we were in sort of a bind back home, which is another story. We'd made a few contacts in Bangkok. Ever been there?"

Kiet shook his head.

Chipperfield winked. "You're a bachelor, right? You oughta boogie on over for a weekend. It's a single guy's wet dream. One night I'll never forget, we scored these two cuties at—"

"Your Bangkok contacts, please."

"You'd be surprised how many Luongans live in Thailand. Some of those boys are on a long string. They know how to grease the skids with the home team and they're sniffing to cut themselves a red-hot deal."

Kiet closed his eyes. Chipperfield's relentless barrage of slang was giving him a headache. "To the essence, please. Sometime soon."

"Okay, fine. This one guy we drank with in Bangkok's finer watering holes, he was tighter'n a tick with Ridsa. We got to talking. What we were good at was simpatico with what he was good at. He got on the horn with the führer, who buzzed in and smoked and joked with us for three days of business and pleasure, Kiet, that you cannot believe. The rest is history."

"The name of the simpatico tight tick?"

Chipperfield jabbed the fingers of one hand into the palm of the other. "Time out. Uh-uh. Ridsa, that prick with ears, he's made it perfectly clear that's confidential, him and us."

"May I guess?"

Chipperfield shrugged. "Free country."

"Fop Tia, Hickorn's previous mayor."

"The human leisure suit. Give the man a cigar."

"Yes or no?"

"Didn't I just say? Yeah."

"Is Fop Tia presently in Hickorn?"

"Is he? I don't know, but you're acting like he is."

"Where would he be staying if he were?"

"Beats me."

"Minister Ridsa, your business associate, might know."

"Might," Chipperfield agreed. "Might."

"You will inquire?"

"We're moving into payback time, Kiet. You know, information for protection."

"My jail is the safest locale in Hickorn."

"No way, José. This kid's not gonna be locked in with a bunch of filthy perverts, eating fish heads and rice. C'mon, escort me onto an airplane."

"No airplane," Kiet said.

"I'm sincere, man. You tapped the well dry."

"A compromise, then."

"I'm listening."

"Your Hickorn Continental room, an armed guard posted outside your door day and night."

Chipperfield paused to think, tugging an ear. "Well, Bangkok'd be better."

"Fish heads and rice and filthy perverts would be worse."

"Yeah, but your idea of protection is same-same as house arrest."

"Confinement is often a state of mind."

"You're going Oriental inscrutable on me again, right? Okay, fine. One condition."

"Yes?"

"We hold off an hour and watch the second 'Gunsmoke.' The networks back home, they don't put quality shows like that on the tube anymore. Deal?"

Kiet smiled and said, "Deal."

12

Bamsan Kiet deposited Chick Chipper-
field at his Hickorn Continental room, requisitioned a
sentry from Headquarters, and drove home at an unsafe
speed, lamenting the unfair quirks and twists of the job
that forever nibbled at the edges of his off-duty time.
Captain Binh had an applicable adage: life's a bitch.

The bitch truism also applied to the show Kiet began
watching, "The Life and Legend of Wyatt Earp." How
could such a slick and manicured and dapper marshal
effectively police Dodge City, which was Matt Dillon's town
anyway? How could a string-tie, pomade-hair swell elicit
respect from uncouth frontier villagers?"

Perhaps a lightning gun hand, an accurately lethal Colt
.45 Peacemaker discharging. The certainty of sanitized
violence kept him from switching off the receiver in disgust
and going to bed. Kiet knew the writers had scripted a
gratifying showdown. American television, he thought.
They had perfected the fantasy of swift justice.

Kiet answered a knock at his door.

"Twice in one day I barge in on you unannounced," said

Madame Mai. "Please accept my deepest apologies. I would not be intruding into your home if my purpose were not important."

When she stopped speaking, she bowed slightly as she had in Ambassador Dang's chambers. A respectful gesture, yes, Kiet thought, but humility did not become her. Puzzled, he invited her inside and to his sofa. They sat at opposite ends.

In place of the prim *áo dèi*, she was wearing black pajamas, standard apparel of the ferocious Vietcong guerrillas. This attire, however, did not appear to be field issue. The garment was too glossy, the tailoring too meticulous. The outfit was loose without being baggy, except at vital latitudes where it was tight yet not clinging.

"I must apologize again for my informal manner of dress," Mai said as she sat. "I received a communiqué from Hanoi and rushed without delay to you."

Kiet blushed. Mia had caught him staring at her Tropics of Cancer and Capricorn. He shut off the television and asked, "May I, uh, bring you a refreshment?"

"Oh, no. No, thank you. Let me tell you what I have to say. Then I will remove my interloping self from your home. Our soccer squad is flying in tomorrow instead of the day after."

Kiet groaned. "Why, please?"

"Our leaders have decided that the team will be safer if their schedule is altered. One might debate that a day after the announced date is preferable to a day before, the team being exposed in Luong for two fewer days."

"One might debate that," Kiet agreed glumly. "Yours truly included. I lose a preparation day."

"Potential troublemakers lose their choice venues."

"Excuse me?"

"Any schemers will have planned elaborately and far in advance. Except for the Savhanakip parade, we regard the airport arrival and the motorcade to our embassy as the

96

least defensible contingencies. We will take them by surprise."

Them, Kiet thought. These foreigners and their obsession with conspiracies. "Would not a day after be equally surprising?"

"A sapper unit in position could just wait."

Yes, Kiet thought, if it were a rural ambush. But madmen laden with satchel charges and rifles, standing fast for twenty-four hours in a city, might be a trifle conspicuous. He was starting to understand the labyrinthine Vietnamese logic. Decades of jungle warfare had rendered the world an unpredictable arena of parry and thrust.

"We shall be ready," Kiet said. "I hope."

Mai rose and walked to the door. Kiet thought she was leaving, but she looked out the window, and then sat back down, closer to the center of the sofa than the far edge, "Does that old American automobile belong to you?"

"A police impound in temporary storage," Kiet said.

"You have a lovely home," she said, her eyes wandering around the room. "In Vietnam, three families would occupy such a spacious villa."

Mai's absence of further curiosity about Chipperfield's Chrysler was curious. "I am indeed fortunate."

"Your wife and children are away tonight?"

"I live alone."

"I'm sorry. I don't mean to snoop into your personal life."

Kiet had the feeling that she was not snooping, that she already knew. Nevertheless, he revealed, "I was once married. Tien died in the cholera epidemic of 1966. We lived here. We had no children."

"I'm sorry."

"I will tolerate no further apologies," Kiet said with mock firmness. "Ambassador Dang mentioned that you were widowed too."

"Yes. Thanh was killed at Hue in 1968."

"I'm sorry," Kiet said.

Mai shook her head. "No sorrow lingers. I remember him joyously. Thanh died a hero of our socialist struggle. He and his regiment lost the battle and Thanh lost his life, but he took many, many imperialist soldiers with him. More than twenty years of widowhood for you and me, Kiet. It must agree with us."

"Yes and no," Kiet said with a hand flutter. She was leading him onto dark, rough terrain, territory that even after all the years had been explored only superficially. The drift of the conversation was reminding him that it had been months since his last "relationship," as Binh termed sexual friendship.

"The freedom is good, yes? The loneliness—sometimes terrible."

He looked over at her to reply, to agree, but she was right there. They kissed and pawed and groped, she fumbling for his zipper, he yanking at silk, silently cursing as he heard the material tear. He was fast and clumsy, an overgrown adolescent, erupting in what seemed a fraction of a second.

They lay entwined on the sofa, saying nothing, breathing heavily, dabbling perspiration droplets from each other's faces with fingertips. He suppressed an apology and she won his gratitude by not patronizing him with a compliment on his manly prowess.

By and by, he sat up, gently removed the rest of her clothing, then his own. He lifted Mai and carried her to his bedroom, imagining Matt and Miss Kitty. This would be Matt's technique, the *beginning* of a masterful seduction. No ripped silk and impatient penetration for Mr. Dillon.

They enjoyed the smallest of small talk, soon combining delicate, exploratory caresses with the chitchat.

"On one hand I can count the number of men I have slept with since Thanh," Mai said. "I have often thought that there is something wrong with me, I'm so seldom attracted. I never thought I would want anybody but a Vietnamese."

"Ambassador Dang told me that Vietnamese and Luongans are brothers in skin and soul."

Mai laughed. "You Luongans are very light-skinned and your noses are skinny."

"I have not failed to notice that Vietnamese are dark and broad-nosed."

"Your eyes are rounder," Mai countered.

"Fuller breasts," Kiet said, fondling them.

Mai straddled him and pushed his hands away. "Don't do anything."

Had he said something that inflamed her? What? He obeyed and they moved in leisurely unison, Mai's eyes closed in some private ecstasy. She finished a beat ahead of him. She turned on a side and pulled his free hand around her, clasping it to a breast.

She was satiated, through with him. He listened to her snoring for a moment and also fell asleep, as if drugged by an entire case of Golden Tiger. Morning sunlight glowing on curtains awakened him. Madame Mai Le Trung was gone.

Somehow he knew she would be.

13

The following morning, at 11:05, a twin-engined turboprop airliner with Aeroflot markings touched down and taxied to an apron adjacent to Hickorn International's terminal. An access road between the terminal and a hangar led directly to Richard Nixon Boulevard, the thoroughfare that united the airport and the city. Because of the short notice, Kiet had persuaded customs to waive check-in procedures. The Vietnamese national soccer team would not be required to queue inside a crowded building, submitting to interviews, baggage searches, and possible danger. If the athletes were smuggling contraband into the Kingdom of Luong, so be it.

Kiet stood with Captain Binh outside the perimeter of official greeters and watched the Vietnamese players march single file out of the Soviet aircraft. They were dressed in the colors of their country's flag: red sweat suits, bold yellow stars emblazoning the tops. These were supple and rugged young men. Not one of them was smiling. The set of their jaws stated their mission.

Luong's fun-loving side smiled too easily and had an

affinity for postpractice camaraderie at bars and coffee-houses. Perhaps a victory next year, Kiet thought. Perhaps we can challenge Antarctica.

"I'm afraid our boys are up to their asses in alligators," Binh said.

Bloody torsos on a soccer pitch? Kiet let it pass. He observed a brief and informal ceremony of hand shaking, unnatural smiles, and applause. Dignitaries had been assembled in haste and most fell into the middle categories of power. Minister of Tourism Ridsa. The foreign minister's second-in-command. A smattering of deputies from other ministries. The porky, cigarette-smoking Ambassador Dang and his entourage. Several military officers, none above the rank of lieutenant colonel.

Madame Mai appeared at his side. "Everything looks under control here, Superintendent."

Keep it stiff and businesslike, Kiet told himself; Binh will never suspect. He pointed to a bus the team was now boarding and said, "Officers on motorbikes will lead and trail it to your embassy. More men are stationed along the route, on the alert for troublemakers."

"Very impressive. I will not worry."

Until this party is over, I *will* worry, he thought. He had pulled a considerable number of men from normal patrol assignments to protect the Vietnamese. Kiet, an agnostic, prayed to any god who would listen that his city not be looted in the meantime. "I am just doing my job, Madame," he said in his most officious voice.

"And thank you again for accommodating us. I must rejoin my delegation. Can we meet later to plan security for the remainder of their stay?"

Kiet nodded crisply and Mai returned to her people. Binh asked, "How did you learn about the switcheroo, Superintendent? You informed me this morning."

The suspicion Kiet had hoped to avoid was tattooed on Binh's furrowed forehead. A callow youth, naive in so many

102

ways, but not in the psychic language of lovers. "She, uh, came to my home last night."

"Oh," Binh said, studying the horizon.

"I was not at Headquarters when the communiqué was received at their embassy," he went on. "Protocol required her to contact me and no one else."

"Sure," Binh said, nodding. "No problem."

Kiet did not reply. He construed in Binh's remote gaze equal portions of envy and repugnance. His superior had bedded a beautiful and exotic woman; his superior had bedded an exotic and beautiful communist, an agent of an aggressive neighbor nation.

Since Tien's death, Kiet's sexuality had swung crazily between phases of promiscuity and celibacy. When he was younger, Luongan women regarded his size and girth as Buddhalike and, therefore, extremely desirable. Of late, his periods of celibacy had extended into a life-style. The disorder of indiscriminate conquest consumed too much energy and was vaguely degrading.

So why after months of chastity was he permitting Binh to toss these jabs of guilt? A man and a woman had merely devoted an evening to basic and long-neglected needs. What was the harm? If anything, the hormonal balance of both was improved, overall health invigorated.

Binh's censure simmered under Kiet's collar. Worse than the silent rebuke was reversal of the father and son flavor that seasoned their friendship. Would Binh next place him on curfew and demand his car keys?

Kiet sought to restore order to the universe. "Developments, please," he said harshly.

He succeeded. Binh flinched. Forehead skin unfurled. "Selkirk and the you-know-what, zilch, sir. Your hunch on Dr. Chi could be the break we've been looking for."

"Gambling?"

"Yes, Superintendent."

"Too many ears nearby," Kiet said. "Come."

They walked through dust motes raised by the bus to the parking lot and Kiet's Citroën. Binh said, "Mr. Lee."

"Ah," Kiet said. Mr. Lee was a Chinese who operated Hickorn gambling dens. His principal wares were dice and cards, but he was reputed to accept wagers on almost anything. Binh had not referred to him as "Mister" out of respect. Lee's first name was unknown.

"I got a line on him because he's branched out into shylocking."

"Excuse me?"

"Loansharking, Superintendent."

"Usurious moneylenders?"

"Same-same."

"Accounts kept in pockets? Collection agencies in the form of Cro-Magnon types with hardwood clubs stuffed in their belts?"

"You got it."

"Why this diversification? I thought Mr. Lee was peaceful and content with games of chance."

"He's still relatively peaceful. There's no big trouble yet that I'm aware of. He's got *beaucoup* cash and has invested a chunk in TVs."

"Mr. Lee is buying and selling television receivers?"

"Uh-uh. Financing them. Everybody in town wants one, you know. His rates are exorbitant, but if you borrow from Mr. Lee you can have a Sony in your home right now."

"Television," Kiet muttered. "Progress."

"So far, he's restricted his loans to good risks, Superintendent. His customers pay through the nose for two or three years, but they're good for it. I don't anticipate violence, but I didn't tell Mr. Lee that when I interviewed him."

"A worthwhile interview, I presume."

Binh grinned. "Oh, yes."

"The context of your interview was the ambiguities of the Hickorn ordinance book? Strict interpretations of consumer finance laws that could admit him to our humble jail?"

"How did you know, Superintendent?"

Kiet smiled. "I trained you. Mr. Lee and Dr. Chi, please."

"Chi's into Lee for an arm and a leg."

"Alligators," Kiet said.

"Huh?"

"Poised to devour Dr. Chi's extremities?"

"Yeah. Okay. I get it. It seems that mild-mannered Dr. Chi has an expensive vice. He's a compulsive gambler and he's on a losing streak. For the past six months, he hasn't been able to draw the right card to save his soul. He's been playing on credit."

"Splendid work, Captain. How much does Dr. Chi owe?"

"I couldn't pin Lee down to a bottom line, but it's got to be humongous."

"Lee never impressed me as being a patient man."

"He isn't. That's the thing. Lee's been leaning on him. Two weeks ago, Chi promised that he'd pay off his markers."

"The complete debt?"

"Yeah."

"Has he?"

"No, but he's convinced Lee that he has a windfall of some kind coming down real soon."

"Did you happen to insert Unknown Asia Tours into the conversation?"

"Sure did. Lee played dumb and I'm halfway inclined to accept his ignorance act. But if Chipperfield and Selkirk ripped off the Golden Peacock in collusion with Chi, there's the windfall."

"Indeed."

"Superintendent, I think the time's ripe to bring Chi in for questioning."

"I agree."

"And give him a polygraph examination?"

How can I refuse in the face of this excellent piece of police work? Kiet thought. "Of course," he said. "I insist."

14

"This is *not* our polygraph, Superintendent."

Captain Binh had just taken it out of the shipping carton. The machine was a rectangular metal box. On its top was a button and a dial. Two insulated wires were taped together, one end obviously designed to plug into a socket on the side of the box. The wires were split at the other end, attached individually to contact points on a plastic strap that fastened with a buckle, like a miniature belt.

"Sorry, but my recollection of the former polygraph is obscure," Kiet said truthfully.

"Ours was state-of-the-art, Superintendent. It had adjustment knobs, chest tubes, galvanic finger sensors, and a graph printer. There's been a terrible mistake."

Kiet examined the machine closely. Affixed to its bottom was a sticker: PROPERTY OF BLENHEIM DEPENDENCY CENTER. OTTUMWA, IOWA.

"Dependency Center," Kiet said. "An orphanage? What need would an orphanage have for a lie revealer machine? Use of it on waifs seems severe."

"I don't know," Binh said in a whining timbre that hurt

Kiet's molars. "Without chest tubes, you can't read respiratory and cardiovascular patterns. Perspiration irregularity is impossible to detect without finger sensors."

Kiet shrugged his shoulders in acceptance of Binh's technical babble. "Perhaps the old machine was obsolete. Progress, Captain. Maybe they have inadvertently sent us the latest, most streamlined model that does its duty with a single attachment to the criminal."

"I don't know," Binh repeated. "Our old polygraph was *so* sophisticated. This gizmo looks like a goddamn toy."

They were outside the interrogation room, where an uncooperative Dr. Latisa Chi awaited. Without benefit of the polygraph, Kiet and Binh had questioned him about the Golden Peacock theft. They had decided to probe on that subject before introducing the Selkirk murder.

Chi related his original story by rote: Ridsa's lecture delayed the National Museum's 4:30 closing time; Ridsa and group left by 5:15; Chi locked up and set alarms at 5:30; Chi discovered the loss the following morning.

The questions were accusatory and Chi had withstood the onslaught well. Upon mention of Mr. Lee and gambling debts, Chi became defiant, demonstrating a surprisingly stout backbone. This transformation from weakling to hard case was instinctive, Kiet knew; the desperation of a man backed to a chasm.

"Well" Kiet said. "It is your gizmo, your choice. Shall we?"

"Yeah, what the hell. Let's go for it," Binh said with a sigh of resignation. "Any polygraph is 90 percent accurate on normal people and 67 percent on sociopaths. This piece of tin might not register every response, but it's better than a poke in the eye with a sharp stick. Oops, one thing. I'll be right back."

The young adjutant went into the interrogation room and Kiet pondered the pertinence of mutilation in the lie-revealing process. Binh came out carrying Dr. Chi's shoes and said, "The polygraph is an emotion detector, Superintendent. In the District of Columbia, experienced suspects hid thumbtacks inside their shoes. They'd step down when they were telling the truth. Pain registered and gave a false reading, same as if they were lying. The results were impossible to evaluate."

The lad was so smug. He was once again flaunting his America-acquired police science know-how. A tiny personality flaw, Kiet told himself. Such a tiny flaw. "Splendid, Captain. I would never have guessed. Are we ready?"

"We are," Binh said, "but I don't know about the good doctor."

The good doctor was not ready, not when he saw the metal box Captain Binh and Superintendent Kiet brought into the interrogation room. He looked at the dangling wires and the miniature belt and its buckle, and folded his arms, burrowing hands into armpits.

The room smelled of perspiration. It was windowless and painted a depressing gray. It was furnished with a steel table, padded wooden swivel chairs for interviewers, and a metal stool for the suspect. Dangling over the table was a bare light socket with the brightest incandescent bulb available in Hickorn. Bamsan Kiet had been the interior decorator. He prohibited physical abuse, but had no objection if the milieu raised unwarranted anxieties.

"Dr. Chi," Kiet said. "We must talk further."

"What is that—a torture device?"

"A harmless police science tool, I assure you. A polygraph. You swear that your replies have been candid. I have strong doubts. This machine will vindicate you if you are being truthful and I will happily apologize to you for your ordeal."

"I am a Luongan citizen. I refuse to submit a minute longer to your medieval inquisition."

Chi's words were squeaky and quavering. His defiance is eroding, Kiet thought. "An inappropriate comparison," he

109

said. "Although your crime is ageless, this is the twentieth century, not the sixteenth. Allow me to say, please, that as a university scholar you should have sprinkled mathematics and statistics courses into your history and philosophy regimen."

"A stupid riddle that makes no sense, Kiet."

Kiet leaned forward on the table, on his elbows, until Chi's darting eyes met his. "My riddle is not nearly as stupid as playing against the house and thinking you can win, Doctor. Mr. Lee doesn't even have to cheat you. Odds and probabilities inherent in his games suffice. You blithely cheat yourself."

"Stupid," Chi said. "Insipid. Moronic. Idiotic."

Binh was in the meantime buckling the polygraph strap to a scrawny forearm. Dr. Chi's intellectual resistance had degenerated to verbal abuse and his physical resistance was nil. Kiet was content to let Binh take over, which he did, explaining in a monotone surely aped from a District of Columbia civil servant the function of the machine, the importance of answering yes or no to each and every question, and not to worry.

Binh commenced the polygraph interrogation. "Is your name Latisa Chi?"

"Yes."

"Are you curator of the National Museum?"

"Yes."

"Have you ever been to the moon?"

"No."

"Are you implicated in the disappearance of the Golden Peacock?"

"No."

Binh gave Kiet a sudden side glance. Kiet knew why. The needle in the dial had not moved from its pin, had not quivered. Perhaps the substitute gizmo *was* a toy. Stupid, insipid, moronic, idiotic. Kiet answered with an oblique nod that said to proceed.

110

"Do you play cards and dice at Mr. Lee's gambling dens?"

Kiet pushed the button by the dial. The dial's needle jumped. So did Dr. Chi.

"*Aieeeow!*"

"Pain?" Kiet asked.

Binh scratched his temple. "Hm, maybe we have a short circuit. Couldn't be a whole lot of juice. One more try. Dr. Chi, do you play cards and dice at Mr. Lee's gambling dens?"

"No," Chi said quickly.

Kiet pushed the button.

"*Owwwoh!*"

"Damn," Binh said, pounding the table. "Not only do they ship us the wrong polygraph, the damn thing is defect—"

"Yes," Chi cried. "I do, I do! My dice have been falling as if they were thrown by the devil himself. I vow that I didn't intend to dishonor the memory of Prince Savhana. If everything had gone according to plan, the Golden Peacock would be ransomed and home."

The police officers were open-mouthed, stunned speechless. Binh's Western police science gadget was indeed a lie revealer, Kiet thought. He poised a crooked finger above the machine and said, "Please continue, Doctor."

The curator's eyes were watery and demented. He was massaging his forearm. "Certainly, yes, I will, I beg you to cease. I—I made a bargain with Selkirk to steal the Golden Peacock."

"Just Selkirk? Not Chipperfield too?" Kiet asked as he gently rapped a fingernail tattoo on the magical button.

"My negotiations were with Selkirk exclusively, but I presume Chipperfield was in his confidence. Chipperfield is a simpleton. I would never have proposed the kidnapping to him."

"Kidnapping?"

"The pricelessness of the Golden Peacock, gentlemen. Is the terminology not appropriate?"

"Go on," Kiet said.

"After Minister Ridsa and his lecture group departed, I moved the treasure to a filing cabinet in Minister Ridsa's office. If the Americans were going to trick me or if the plan went awry for any reason, my culpability would be minimal. Minister Ridsa, a cretin *and* a bully, would bear the blame. I had given Selkirk duplicate keys. I deliberately neglected to activate the alarm when I left for the day. Selkirk was to enter the National Museum at a late hour, manufacture the break-in evidence—the gouge marks on the alarm box, the cut-out window pane, the alarm tape bypass—and remove the Peacock. Then he was to contact the Royal Palace and elicit a ransom fee. The deed would be accomplished, the money divided between Selkirk and myself. I concede that my rationalization was slender and venal, but I sincerely believed that the unseemly transaction would be completed secretly and expeditiously. Nobody would be the wiser and the only damage would be a comparatively trifling decrease of Royal Treasury funds."

"But something did go awry," Kiet said.

"Alas, yes. Selkirk notified me the following morning in rather blunt language that he had entered the National Museum and fabricated the burglary sham. He claimed that the Peacock was *not* in Minister Ridsa's filing cabinet. I was skeptical."

"Are you presently skeptical?"

"No."

"Because of Mr. Selkirk's murder?"

"Yes. I cannot prove it, but I believe Minister Ridsa returned to his office for some reason and realized the alarm was off. He saw that the Peacock was gone and looked about. I may have disturbed something in his office when I hid the icon. I was terribly nervous. I have never before committed a crime."

"Except participating in illegal games of chance," Kiet reminded him.

"I needed a large sum of money. Dr. Lee threatened to break my kneecaps if the debt was not soon paid."

"Gamblers and shylocks do that, Superintendent," Binh said.

"Was the theft your brilliant inspiration or Selkirk's?"

Chi shook his head. "I cannot candidly say. He and I talked at length one evening and it—it rose out of the conversation."

"What do you know of the murder?"

"I didn't kill him. I didn't. I—"

"I know," Kiet said, remembering Chipperfield's claim that Ridsa had called Selkirk. "You are not the violent type. Tell me, please, how did you happen to be the one who found Selkirk's body?"

"Earlier that evening, Minister Ridsa telephoned me at home. He was extremely angry. He claimed that he had been working late. Upon his departure he saw that the museum was dark, that every light was off.

"I was certain that I had kept lights in the outer rooms on. One could not peer in at the Peacock exhibit, but the lighting was adequate to discourage another burglary. In my state of apprehension, though, I conceded that I could have been remiss. Evidently I was. I went to the museum. The lights were off. I went inside and saw . . . Mr. Selkirk."

"Anything else?"

"No. Positively not. What is to become of me? What?"

Kiet motioned Binh to disconnect the polygraph, then rocked in his padded wooden swivel chair, staring at the gray walls, presenting the illusion of deep and grave thought. He already knew what he was going to do, but he bided his time. The illusion, the delay, was for the benefit of the man perched on the metal stool. It was an illusion of contemplated arrest and confinement, of possible summary justice. Who could predict the superintendent's righteous fury? Matt handled his Dodge City marshal's business in the very same manner. Strong, silent, stoic. Dissolving every last speck of criminal resistance.

Chi bowed his head. "You have my full and unequivocal cooperation, Superintendent Kiet. I will even sign a confession without reading it. I deserve to rot in prison."

Splendid! Kiet thought, withholding his emotions. "We will prepare a statement for you to sign, Dr. Chi. There is a problem, however. You are confessing to the theft of an object that is not officially stolen."

"Yes?"

"What is the word I am seeking, Captain? Retroactive?"

Binh winked good-naturedly. "Close enough for government work."

"You will remain at your National Museum post for now, Doctor," Kiet said. "You will be on duty twenty-four hours a day under house arrest. You will be supervising plumbing and electrical repairs, working around the clock to ensure completion of building restoration in time for Savhanakip. You will maintain this beneficial fraud. You must not fail, you must not—"

"Let the cat out of the bag," Binh interrupted.

"Whatever," Kiet said. "Agreed?"

The perspiration-drenched Dr. Latisa Chi uncoiled what muscles he had, slumping on the metal stool like Jell-O removed from its mold. His lips turned upward in a pathetic copy of a smile. "Agreed," he said. "Agreed, agreed, agreed."

C h i ' s confession document was too confidential to assign to a stenographic clerk-typist. Binh lugged in a leaden and ancient Underwood typewriter—the department's finest—and attempted to transfer the information to paper. His hunt-and-peck method was interminable. Entire seconds separated thunking keystrokes.

Kiet impatiently scribbled the gist onto a pad and handed it to Chi for his signature. Binh compared Kiet's handwriting to what might be found on a scroll in a tomb, a lifetime career of translation ahead for the archaeologist. Chi had, after all, said he wouldn't bother reading what was offered him. Following an incredulous squint at the notepad, he signed, true to his word.

Before they drove the curator to his museum/jail, Binh asked Kiet whether it was okay to check out the polygraph glitch first. Did they have time? Kiet sighed and said of course; Savhanakip was three days away and seventy-two hours was an eternity.

Kiet's sarcasm missed its target. It was as if he had fired a blank. They took the machine to Kiet's office. Binh buckled the strap to his own wrist, plugged it in, and pushed the magical lie-revealing button. He winced slightly, a masculine wince, and said, "Weak voltage, Superintendent. I suppose Chi has a low threshold of pain. He would."

"I suppose," Kiet said.

Binh pushed the button again. Then again. "Same-same. I wouldn't want to do this for a living, but it's no big deal and the zap doesn't vary. It's like this gizmo was actually made to jolt you."

"Perhaps," Kiet said.

"Boy, if I was an inventor, I'd make a lot of bucks on this thing."

"Excuse me?"

"You know, it would be perfect to break bad habits. Say a guy can't stop smoking or drinking. Give him a cigarette or a shot of booze. Whenever he takes a puff or a swig, he gets a zing. He'd be clean in nothing flat."

Such an active imagination, Kiet thought. "Amazing," he said to be polite. "Who knows what modern science will dream of next?"

15

K i e t a n d B i n h transferred one house-arrest prisoner (Dr. Latisa Chi) to the National Museum in the Citroën and went to the Hickorn Continental Hotel to visit their other (Mr. Chick Chipperfield). What a nice police superintendent I am, Kiet thought. What nice jails I provide for major felons.

That thought was bitter and brief. The puzzle that preoccupied him during Binh's rabid chauffeuring was Phorn Ridsa's niche in the mess. Kiet would confidently wager a year's salary with Mr. Lee that Ridsa had killed Selkirk. But why? And how could he prove it?

The Golden Peacock burglary was the enigma. Binh's lie revealer had driven mild, unintentional voltage through the body of a man who could not endure pain. Kiet would confidently wager another year's salary with Mr. Lee that Chi's confession was truthful to the letter.

Hence: Ridsa had accidentally stumbled upon the theft and dealt himself in. He was a secondary player, the beneficiary of a godsend, of loaves and fishes, a latecomer who was extemporaneously revising the rules of the game.

Kiet hated unpredictability in his criminals. The unswerving, generic greed of the Selkirk-Chipperfield(?)-Chi alliance was fundamental. They were amateur thieves. The crime could—yes, *would*—have been solved long before Savhanakip. But no. Not now. Not with the wildly ambitious Phorn Ridsa joining in on the fun. Not with the uncoincidental coincidence of Ridsa's compatriot, Fop Tia, appearing on Luongan soil.

Bamsan Kiet, burdened by these brain twisters, was in a mood darker than a total eclipse when he and Binh entered the Continental and headed for the main staircase and Chick Chipperfield's luxurious jail cell.

"Superintendent!"

Kiet turned around. Gaston LaCroix, the Continental's manager, a dazzling and baggy white in his Sydney Greenstreet suit, scuttled toward them as fast as his brittle bones would allow. He was waving a sheet of paper.

"Ah," Kiet said. "Information?"

"No. Not in the context of our last discussion, if that is what you mean."

Kiet raised a hand. "Later, please."

LaCroix proffered the sheet of paper. "It is vitally important, Superintendent, that we—"

Kiet saw columns of numbers on the paper. "Do not pester me again until you see evil, hear evil, and speak evil, LaCroix."

Anger and frustration had constricted Kiet's throat. His words were barely audible. They were guttural—scarcely words at all. LaCroix jerked back the paper, as if Kiet were electrified.

Binh and Kiet went up the stairs to Chipperfield's second-floor room. The guard at the door snapped to attention. Kiet asked him, "Has he had visitors?"

"No, sir, except uniformed hotel people bringing meals. Waiters, waitresses, and a man wearing a suit and tie who said he was an assistant manager. As ordered, I search everyone for weapons."

"Did you recognize them?"

"I don't know the employees, Superintendent, but they all had food and drink."

Kiet opened the door and went in. Chipperfield was on the bed, hands folded behind his head. "Hey, don't you guys believe in knocking?"

Kiet ignored the criticism of his manners and looked around. The room was filthy, dishes and glasses and trays and clothing scattered randomly. It had a rank, clinging odor of stale food, liquor, and—oddly, for how could this be?—sex. The television was on. The Lone Ranger and Tonto were engaged in a choreographed brawl with four criminals. Unrealistic, Kiet thought. Too tidy. You knew the punches weren't landing. Compared to "Gunsmoke," the so-called action was laughable.

Chipperfield stood and brushed crumbs from his glossy bathrobe. "You like? I picked it up in Tokyo. They said pure silk, but your guess is as good as mine. It's like those kimonos. Ever been to Japan, big guy?"

"No."

Chipperfield winked. "Oughta give it a shot. The broads in those places, they walk on your back too."

Captain Binh's nostrils were twitching. "Stinks."

"Yeah, no kidding," Chipperfield said. "Maid service is lousy. You got any pull with LaCroix? You oughta raise holy hell."

Kiet looked at him. "The accommodations are unsatisfactory, Mr. Chipperfield? The alternative of fish heads, rice, and perverts is—"

Chipperfield interrupted with a brittle grin and a violent headshake. "No, hey, don't get me wrong. I'm not bitching. Forget I ran off at the mouth, okay?"

"We had a bargain. Information in exchange for protection."

Chipperfield sighed and pointed at the telephone. "I'm trying. Rome wasn't built in a day, you know."

"Minister Ridsa?"

"Hey, I guess I don't have to clue you in on Hickorn's telephone system. It's easier to send a smoke signal than get through to somebody. I about wore out a finger dialing, but I did get lucky and got through to Ridsa's office. Twice. I left messages."

"Fop Tia?"

"Okay, fine. Ridsa's my pipeline to Tia. If Ridsa's gonna treat me like I got the plague, what do you want me to do? I'm in a cage. My wheelin' and dealin' and mobility is severely limited. I haven't seen or heard from anybody in the fast lane."

Aside from solving the theft and the murder, Kiet did not know what he wanted Chipperfield to do. He traded glances with Binh, signals police officers flash to one another when deliberating whether their subject is sincere or not. Binh's lips twisted up the port side of his face. A starboard eyebrow raised. Translation: you tell me.

"One dialing finger is abraded," Kiet said. "You have nine others."

Chipperfield spread an uninjured index finger and middle finger in a V, flexed them, and smiled. "I'm a man good for his word, Kiet. Scout's honor. I'm gonna make these fingers do a whole big bunch of walking."

"Please do," Kiet said. He and Binh descended the stairs, skeptical as they could be. LaCroix was waiting at the bottom, a pleading expression on his face. He was holding the vitally important sheet of paper at his side. Kiet granted himself a Dillonesque fantasy. The paper was a Colt .45. LaCroix quick-drew it. Kiet slapped leather, beat LaCroix by a millisecond, and shot the Colt out of the varmint's hand.

"Very well," Kiet said. "If we must."

LaCroix gave him the paper, which proved to be a

running tally of room service charges for the past eighteen hours. Kiet groaned. Nearly one hundred thousand zin. Dinners, snacks, alcoholic beverages, generous tips. On two occasions, drinks had been delivered by LaCroix's *terrrasse* "hostesses," with charges increased accordingly.

"Mr. Chipperfield instructed me that he is in the custody of the Hickorn Police Department and that you are compensating us for his board," LaCroix said. "Is this an accurate assumption, Superintendent?"

Kiet looked at Binh for clarification of this fine legal point. None was forthcoming. Binh disapproved of house arrest, of coddling vermin who belonged in jail. "It's a gray area," he said blandly.

"We owe him subsistence," Kiet said. "We do not owe him an ongoing orgy."

"But who will pay my bill?"

"You did not monitor his extravagance, LaCroix. I suppose you did not monitor his visitors either."

The prospect of sleazy barter washed a tinge of color onto LaCroix's chalky complexion. "Forgive the tardiness of my aging memory, Superintendent. Now I remember. One and only one nonemployee did visit, a gentleman smartly dressed in suit and tie. I personally observed him entering Mr. Chipperfield's room with a sandwich presumably purchased from a street vendor."

"Do your assistant hotel managers wear suits and ties?"

"No. Blazers and open collars."

"As I thought. The name of the smartly dressed gentleman, please."

"We have never been formally introduced, but I have seen him. Tui Nha."

"The grain broker?"

"Yes."

Ah, a crony of ex-mayor and ex–Bangkok expatriate Fop Tia. Before his entry into politics, Tia had traded and speculated in commodities—lumber, rice, and tobacco.

Kiet thanked LaCroix for his cooperation, pocketed the obscene bill, and dismissed him with a hearty handshake.

"We aren't paying it, are we, Superintendent?" Binh asked.

"No. I would not soil a thirteen-year affiliation with mammon. He will bury the loss in his creative accounting and we will continue to be blinded to embezzlement and prostitution."

"How about Chipperfield?"

"An excellent question," Kiet said.

"His nose is growing clear out to here," Binh said, extending an arm.

"Excuse me?"

"Same as Pinocchio's."

Whatever a Pinocchio is, Kiet thought; please spare me the insight. He said, "Regardless, he lied to us. While I attend to a matter, please place Mr. Chipperfield under arrest on an unspecified warrant. The guard can assist you."

Binh's smile was beatific. "And take him to *our* jail, Superintendent?"

"Yes. If we are out of fish heads and rice and perverts, see if you can obtain some."

T u i Nha Wholesale Ltd. was located on Ma San Boulevard, five blocks south of the river docks. Nha specialized in rice and was Hickorn's largest broker. He bought farmers' paddy in advance and cheaply, at the midpoint of the growing season when impoverished peasants had spent most of the monies received for their previous crops. After harvest, Nha and his counterparts warehoused the grain and meted it out to millers at a substantial profit, keen eyes on the rise and fall of market prices.

Kiet knew the system too well; his rice-farming sister and brother-in-law were perennial victims of this cycle.

Hickorn's ordinance book prohibited hoarding and manipulation of commodities prices, but the offense was virtually impossible to prove. The greed of Nha and the other big brokers was highly disciplined. They had an uncanny feel for trouble, an intuition of the cost per kilo that would send mobs into the streets. They answered unrest before it erupted, reluctantly opening their spigots, thus adjusting supplies to affordable demand. Bamsan Kiet would have gladly swapped five homicide convictions for one open-and-shut case against a rice hoarder.

The front office of Tui Nha Wholesale Ltd. was shabby. Four desks as cluttered with paperwork as Kiet's own sat on dusty concrete. The institutional-green walls were tinted with cigarette smoke and neglect. The ceiling consisted of rafters and upstairs flooring planks. It appeared swayback, presumably due to the weight of fifty-kilo sacks of paddy stored above. The grubbiness was stagecraft, a false image of skimpy profits, a placebo for enraged citizens who occasionally stormed in to protest stiff prices. The mien and Tui Nha's persuasive words usually assuaged. Kiet knew better.

Nha, a natty man in his forties, occupied one of the desks. He looked up and blinked. "Kiet."

"Are you surprised to see me?"

"Of course I am. My rice business isn't police business."

"Perhaps it should be. Where is he, please?"

Nha was as peaceful and emotionless as an embalmed corpse. "Where is who?"

Kiet gestured at him. "You gave yourself away. That splendid sharkskin suit you have on. Nobody so elegant delivers sandwiches."

Nha smiled the boys-will-be-boys smile of a hustler caught fibbing. "I didn't think the sandwich ruse would work, but it was his idea. He asked me to convey condolences for the death of the American's partner."

Fop Tia taking such a risk to express sympathy regarding

123

the departed Doublemint Twin? No, thank you. "Where is he?"

Nha's attention turned to his work, a ledger the size of a dictionary. "Up the steps behind me. The door at the end of the hallway. It's a storeroom I converted into living quarters, which I use when I'm working late. I put him up as a favor. I went to the Continental as a favor. He thinks I'm his errand boy and he's been meddling in my business. We aren't associates any longer, you know. I don't deserve the aggravation. It's not worth creating problems with you, Kiet."

Kiet took the stairs to the room at the end of the hall. The door had no lock and the knob turned easily, but the door resisted. Kiet threw his bulk to it, shoulder first. His weight snapped a wooden chair that had been wedged under the inside knob. The room's lone window faced the alley. It was raised. Plump buttocks and a trailing leg filled the air space.

"Mr. Mayor," Kiet said.

"Shit," Fop Tia said.

Kiet tapped Tia's shoe with a sandal, just hard enough to suggest that it might be kicked out from beneath him. "We are fifteen feet above the ground, sir. There is no fire ladder."

"I could've hung and dropped." Tia extended an arm. "Help me in, will you?"

"The Hickorn Police Department is pledged to aid citizens in distress," Kiet said, taking Hickorn's ex-mayor by the wrist and aiding him with a hard yank.

Tia stumbled in on his heels and fell backward. Kiet caught him and gave him a sidelong shove. Tia landed on the bed, flat on his stomach. "*Ooof!*"

"There," Kiet said. "You are safe."

Tia turned over and sat up. "How did you know I was in Hickorn?"

"I saw you get off the Bangkok shuttle. Conservative suit,

124

goatee, glasses. Same disguise as now." Kiet shook his head. "Fop Tia is Fop Tia. How did you know I was downstairs?"

"An air shaft on the other side of the bed. Nobody else recognized me," Tia said, removing the flat-lens glasses.

"Your constituency has forgotten you. I never will."

"Former constituency, thanks to you. Forgive me if I'm not flattered."

"You had a major hand in destroying Hickorn's economy with counterfeit money, Tia. I did you a favor by chasing you out of Luong. I wish I could have had you blindfolded against sandbags and shot."

Tia smiled. "I was mayor then. I had power. If you had arrested me and taken me before a court of law, it might have been interesting."

It might have been, Kiet thought. Tia was quite capable of suborning the justice process. Arrest and trial was a risk neither man had been willing to take. "I'm interested in the present. Why are you in Hickorn?"

"Business."

"Unknown Asia Tours?"

"What else? My life's savings are invested in a silent partnership."

An unsurprising revelation. "I'm disappointed that I didn't send you into exile as a pauper."

"Don't be too disappointed, Kiet. You took in excess of two hundred thousand American dollars from me. My other assets were a fraction of that. I stand to lose everything."

"Unknown Asia Tours is doing badly?"

Tia spoke, raising three fingers, one at a time. "The hamburger café isn't making a profit. We aren't getting as many tourists as we expected. The TV operation is killing us. Until we can cut through the red tape and get approval from the government to sell advertising time, Channel Seven isn't earning us a zin."

"You can't give up on television," Kiet blurted. "Television is synonymous with progress."

Tia laughed. "You, an advocate of progress?"

Kiet blushed. "Never mind. Why is your partnership suddenly unsilent?"

"Al's murder. Have you solved it yet?"

"No."

"With Al's death compounding our financial reverses, I had to investigate for myself."

"What have you investigated thus far?"

"Not much. As you know, Tui Nha called on Chick for me. That's all I've had time to do."

"And Mr. Chipperfield said?"

"His theory is that the Rouge is undermining us. Do you accept it?"

"No."

"Everyone says that the Golden Peacock is gone. True?"

"No."

"Dr. Chi is next on my list. Do I have your permission to continue an independent investigation? There's a Western expression: two heads are better than one."

Kiet thought of another Western expression, a Binhism: loose cannon. "Absolutely not."

"What are you going to do with me, put me on an airplane and into exile again?"

"I am tempted."

"Listen, Kiet, I'm not a fugitive. You never charged me with a crime. Technically, I'm a free Luongan citizen."

"Technically, yes, but your complicity in the counterfeiting is common knowledge. Thousands and thousands of your fellow free Luongan citizens, your former constituents, were harmed. If they knew you were in Hickorn, their memories might be jogged."

"You would, wouldn't you?"

Kiet did not have to reply.

"You have Chick under house arrest. Tui Nha indicated

126

to me that he was enjoying it. Is that a viable option for me?"

"It is," Kiet said. "Viable and only."

"Here?"

"No. People know you are here. For the moment, it is to my advantage also to keep Fop Tia and his whereabouts a secret. I happen to have learned of a recent vacancy at the Hickorn Continental."

Tia lay down, head on pillow, hands clasped over chubby midsection, eyes on the ceiling. "In the eloquent words of my colleague Chick: Okay, fine."

16

I t   w a s   n o t   l o v e, it was lust. Kiet had inhabited the planet for sufficient years to know the difference. Love was an agonizingly complex emotion. Love required nuances and mutual respect. Love required the enrichment of time. Lust was simpler. Lust was a pleasurable motor-nerve connection between brain and groin.

Following a libidinous weekend with a new lady friend, Binh would tell Kiet with lecherous glee that he had again "fallen in lust." Apropos. Bamsan Kiet had fallen in lust with Mai Le Trung.

That night, after a gymnastic and enervating session with her, Kiet lay in the twilight of sleep, wondering whether Mai had fallen in lust with him. Despite her tender murmurings during lovemaking, he did not yield to self-deception; she was too mature and sophisticated to fall instantly and passionately in love with an overweight, middle-aged Luongan widower. He was more than happy to settle for lust. It appealed to his sense of fair play and to his masculinity.

If his eyes had been completely closed, he would not have

noticed her leave his bed. She flowed out of it without a sound, without even a rustling of linen. He felt a chill, thinking that she must have been a fearsome and deadly Vietcong guerrilla.

He watched in a feigned-sleep squint as she searched the clothing he had worn that day. If he had been in the habit of recording notes on paper rather than in his head, he would have confronted her. She finished her search and left his villa, quiet as a ghost.

He shut his eyes entirely, saddened but unsurprised. Madame Mai was not in love. She was not in lust. She was in espionage.

17

''Superintendent, you look like you just lost your best friend. You look like the world's about to end.''

Binh had come to Kiet's home the next morning to report an overnight riot in the jail. "No, Captain. Only my last vestige of innocence is lost."

"Huh?"

"Never mind. The riot you spoke of, please?"

"Well, maybe *riot* is an exaggeration. The desk sergeant and jailers were really bent out of shape. When I got them to mellow out and sifted the wheat from the chaff, it boiled down to a one-man disturbance. Guess who."

Kiet digested what he could of the rapid-fire slang, sighed, and stepped into his sandals. He was not in the deep depression Binh had implied, but neither was he especially eager to face the emerging day. He was resigned to Mai's sexual motivation, his dismal frame of mind caused more by his own naiveté than her treachery. Compounding his gloom was the electronic fuzz on his television screen. He had turned on the receiver hoping for a western, an inspirational hour of crime-investigation-solution. Evidently it was too early. He rose, switched it off, and said, "Mr. Chipperfield?"

"Right on," Binh said. "He was pissing and moaning all night long. He called you everything but a nice guy. He says our jail is the Black Hole of Calcutta. He's demanding to telephone his embassy and his congressman and '60 Minutes.' He says your ass is grass and Mike Wallace will be the lawnmower."

"Timepieces and gardening equipment?"

"'60 Minutes' is a popular exposé program on American TV, Superintendent."

"Are we abusing Mr. Chipperfield?"

"Nope. He's being treated humanely, like our other prisoners. He's objecting to eating from a communal rice bowl, sleeping on a straw mat, and relieving himself in a hole in the floor."

"Flush toilets and room service. Addictive luxuries," Kiet said. "Am I needed?"

"No, but I thought you should know. I warned him to cool it or we'd have him sedated. He's about burned out anyway. He'll be okay."

"A day or so of reflection in our Black Hole of Calcutta might make him an honest man."

Binh smiled. "That and our polygraph."

"Our other friend, Fop Tia. How is he behaving?"

"Nary a peep. We hustled him up the back stairs to Chipperfield's room. Nobody saw us. LaCroix and I had a meeting of the minds. Tia gets three meals a day and laundry. No booze, no whores, no visitors, no telephone."

"Splendid. Any progress on Selkirk and the Peacock?"

"Zilch," Binh said with a head-shaking frown. "Want to know how I read it?"

"Indeed."

"Chi, Tia, and Chipperfield are giving the bare minimum. They're in a jam with us, so they're going through the motions."

"Please continue."

"They're minor leaguers. Phorn Ridsa is the main man. If he hasn't got the Peacock, I'm Elvis Presley."

"Sideburns," Kiet said. "Blue suede shoes."

"Yeah, and even though the Peacock kind of fell into his lap, you can believe he's made big plans for it. Chi, Tia, and Chipperfield may be afraid of us, but they're a helluva lot more afraid of Ridsa."

"Therefore, what further knowledge they have of the mess will be withheld."

"You're right, unfortunately."

"We can presume that Ridsa is improvising. Whatever he's going to do, he probably can't do it alone. Chi, Tia, and Chipperfield are out of commission, so we can further presume that he is in the market for accomplices."

"Okay, but who?"

Kiet shrugged. "It might be worthwhile to have Ridsa followed."

Binh cleared his throat and said, "Well, I was kind of thinking the same thing. Yesterday I pulled two men off airport surveillance and assigned them to Ridsa. I didn't have anybody else. I would've consulted you first, Superintendent, but you were real busy."

Binh waited nervously for approval. A decision that important should have been *mine* to make, Kiet thought. It was imperative that the Golden Peacock did not fly out of Luong. On the other hand, the redeployment was a good choice. If the treasure was to take wing, Ridsa would be launching it.

Kiet camouflaged his bruised pride with a broad smile. "Excellent, Captain. I applaud your initiative."

Binh beamed. "Thanks. I wish I had some news for you, but so far, zilch. Ridsa hasn't been anywhere except office and home. A two-man surveillance team is usually inadequate, but he's made it easy for them."

Kiet had an idea. He stood and said, "The time is ripe to interview Minister Ridsa."

"And ask what?"

"I don't know. I'll ponder my words en route. Perhaps we can alter his dull schedule."

"By rattling his cage so he'll make a rash move?"

"Hopefully."

"By lying through our teeth?"

"Of course."

"For an occasion like this, we ought to travel in style, Superintendent."

"Excuse me?"

"Chipperfield's land yacht. It is impounded department property, you know."

Binh was still giddy from the praise. And how he loved to sit behind the wheel of an automobile. There was no sensible reason to squelch his euphoria. Kiet said, "You drive."

B i n h twirled an index finger. "With this alone, I steer a two-and-a-half-ton car. Can you imagine, Superintendent? I can push a button on the dashboard and shift gears. Give me a long stretch of freeway and a tap on the gas pedal would goose us up to a hundred easy. Maybe one-ten. Switch your toe to the brake and you're back at zero. No fuss, no muss. No effort, no feel. What a ride this baby has! Before conservation and oil embargoes and air pollution laws, Americans drove these kinds of cars."

"No feel," Kiet agreed. Floating on foam-filled seats and a spongy suspension, he felt weightless, like an orbiting astronaut. He was reminded of Chipperfield's remark about "Old Yellow cutting a swath" through traffic. Binh was doing just that, speeding and substituting his horn for brakes. Pedestrians and cyclists and motorists were remarkably prudent. They yielded the right of way, unwilling to challenge a rolling barge. Kiet felt, if anything, exceptionally safe. His young adjutant could not possibly kill him today.

Kiet and Binh arrived at the Ministry of Tourism/National Museum. No passersby were disputing the CLOSED FOR REPAIRS sign on the museum door. Good. They went into the ministry and asked for Ridsa. The clerk at the reception desk directed them across the street to the old United States embassy building, where the minister was examining office space.

They found the dapper Ridsa on the second floor, holding a clipboard, gazing out the windows of a corner office. He was wearing beige corduroy trousers, a pullover shirt, and white athletic shoes.

Binh pointed at the shoes and said in whispered reverence, "Reeboks."

"Kiet," Ridsa said, turning. "I trust this isn't a social call."

"It isn't," Kiet said. "I have questions and information."

"I'm certain I can't answer any of your questions, but I'll be pleased to hear your information. Does this mean you're finally making headway?"

"Perhaps."

Ridsa wagged a finger. "Fine, but before you begin, come here a minute. I don't like you, Kiet, and every encounter we have decomposes into a confrontation, but I value your opinion. Nothing is official until His Royal Highness signs papers, but I've been given verbal assurances that the Ministry of Tourism will be offered either this northeast section of suites or equal square footage in the southeast section. Look out the windows."

Kiet looked out the windows. "Yes?"

"Well?"

"Excuse me?"

Ridsa closed his eyes and shook his head slowly. "The view, Kiet. The view. This or its southeast duplicate will be my private office, my inner sanctum. As you can see, the National Assembly is the conspicuous landmark. The National Bank is at the southeast. The National Assembly is arguably superior to the National Bank in terms of prestige, but if you press a cheek against the east glass there, you can see a tiny sliver of the Royal Palace. It'd be no contest if the carpeting here weren't fairly new. The southeast's is threadbare. Carpeting versus view has me wavering. What would you do?"

Kiet closed his eyes and shook his head slowly. Ridicule was his intent. Ridsa was the probable murderer of Ambulance Al Selkirk and the possessor of Luong's wondrous icon, the disappearance of which guaranteed in two days a Savhanakip celebration of drunken hysteria and bloodletting. He should have been on guard, on edge, protecting himself and his fiendish visions. He wasn't, not ostensibly. He was instead lost in bureaucratic vanity, consulting Hickorn's chief law enforcement officer about status. Kiet had a new and chilling perception of his adversary.

"I recommend the southeast," he said. "Rugs wear out. Hickorn views do not. Royal Palace views, no matter how slight, do not. It is a case of finite prestige versus infinite prestige."

Ridsa thought for a moment and said, "Sage advice. That's how I'll go."

Kiet suppressed a groan. He had not meant to be sage, he had meant to be cynical.

Ridsa glanced at his watch. "On to your business, Kiet. Be succinct. I'm a busy man."

"Did you know that Fop Tia was in Hickorn for a short period?"

Ridsa squinted. "Tia? The mayor? That Tia?"

That Tia. As if they were distant acquaintances, Kiet thought. "Yes sir. He came in disguise."

"Why should I know? We've lost touch."

"I expect you have. We've been talking to people who

136

were close to him in the past in an attempt to discover the purpose of his return."

Ridsa laughed the laugh of one amused by a jester. "Kiet, forgive me for advising you how to do your job, but why don't you ask Tia?"

Kiet, a man forlorn, lowered his eyes. "We did not get to him in time. He is gone."

"Gone where?"

"Less than an hour ago he boarded an Air France flight, the final destinations of which are Zurich and Paris," Kiet said, sighing. "We missed him by ten minutes."

"Strange," Ridsa said. "How long was he in Hickorn?"

"One to two days."

"Not long," Ridsa said thoughtfully. "What did he do in town?"

"We aren't sure."

"You insinuated that you were making headway in the investigations. Is Fop Tia the headway?"

"Perhaps," Kiet said. "I'm no champion of coincidences."

"Nor I of wishful speculation, Kiet," Ridsa said, attention focused on his clipboard. "Tia is an old enemy of yours. Therefore he kills and steals. Bandits and sociopaths are loose on Hickorn streets. That's where you should be. Quit wasting my time."

Outside, Binh said, "A wonderful performance, Superintendent. He treated you like a dog. If it had been me, I would have lost my cool. I would've blown it."

"I didn't suffer loss of face," Kiet said. "He can spit on me if it leads us to the Golden Peacock. I didn't overact, did I?"

"No. Saying that Tia was observed carrying a Golden Peacock–shaped package onto the airplane would have been overacting. You planted a seed. Ridsa's imagination should take him to the same conclusion."

As they drove away, Kiet looked around. He did not see Binh's two surveillance men. They were either doing their job well or not at all. Let it be the former, Kiet thought. Please.

18

Binh nosed Old Yellow through Headquarters'
gate to parking that had been laid out by the French for
four-wheel vehicles no larger than Renaults and Simcas. At
low speed, back and forth, back and forth, back and forth,
power-steering pump screeching, Binh slipped the Imperial alongside a row of department motorbikes. Kiet got
out, imagining newborn calves and a water buffalo with
chromium nipples.

The reception area was in an uproar. Four handcuffed
youths and twice that number of uniformed officers were
at the front desk. Two policemen and all four young men
were bloodied. With the exception of a handcuffed kid—
early twenties at the oldest—whose nose favored one side
of his face, none appeared to be seriously injured. The
dozen combatants were simultaneously shouting their ver-
sions of the misunderstanding at the booking sergeant,
who had cupped his ears.

Kiet smelled liquor fumes and adrenaline. He touched
Binh's arm and tilted his head toward the melee, language

that bespoke the prerogative of rank: Dispose of the mess and enlighten me when you have.

He went into his office, looked at his desk, and groaned. Heaps of paper obscured the surface, like snowdrifts in an arctic storm. The press of the Golden Peacock and Selkirk investigations had been an excuse to ignore this bureaucratic torture. He was in the field, engrossed in genuine police work. If there was justice in the universe, a serene balance of yin and yang, the paper flow should have slowed. But it had not. The blizzard was unending.

Kiet segregated documents and memoranda, thinking what a contrast his desk was to Matt's. The only papers he had seen in the Dodge City marshal's office were "wanted" posters. It was soon evident that Savhanakip was responsible for the cosmological disorder. Incident Report form upon Incident Report form made up the tallest pile. By custom older than Kiet, some Hickorn citizens began celebrating Savhanakip a day or two or five prior. Workers sent wives and children and friends to employers with tales of viruses, vapors, and incapacitating muscular aches. Others wheedled out of their shops, cafés, and factories early, citing infections contracted from their absent co-workers. Employers themselves were not immune to the epidemic.

Thankfully the malingerers were a minority, Kiet thought as he scanned the reports. Hickorn was no industrious microcosm of Tokyo or New York. If everyone decided to frolic, his city might well congeal into an inertia from which it would never recover.

Too many incidents, though. Many too many. Double last year's. Alcohol and/or opium a factor in seventy percent, no, eighty percent of them. Nobody seemed to be having any fun either. Family fights. Barroom bravado. Bicycle and pedicab collisions. Vendors and customers pushing and shoving and kicking over the price of mangoes. A man urinating from a balcony. Two prostitutes settling the

140

sovereignty of a street corner with fingernails, obscenities, and saliva. A barber roughly sheared with his own scissors by an intoxicated client who claimed too much had been taken off the sides.

Stop, Kiet said to himself. Cease. He pushed the reports to a desktop corner. He perused messages. From Ambassador Smithson. From functionaries of three different ministries. From Lin Aidit at Unknown Asia Tours, the only one not marked URGENT. He stuffed the last in his pocket as Captain Binh walked in.

"A routine scuffle for the most part," he said. "The boy with the broken nose is half Vietnamese. He was in a café on Rue Ne Win drinking beer. The three other guys were at a table next to him. They got into a beef over the soccer match. The boy said the Viets would beat us by seven goals."

"Then came the eruption."

"Nope. The football thing was pretty good-natured. All hell broke loose when the half-breed repeated a rumor."

"Dare I ask?"

"That Prince Pakse stole the Golden Peacock and is sneaking off to France."

Kiet shut his eyes and rubbed them, as if to erase all images of the past week. "Disposition, please?"

"We're issuing written warnings and releasing them on the condition they pay for damages to the café. We can't jail them. We have no room. Which reminds me, Chipperfield is venting steam again."

"It's time for a chat," Kiet said.

Binh smiled. "In the interrogation room?"

Kiet said of course. Binh brought Chipperfield there and perched him on the metal stool.

"It has been too long," Kiet said.

Chipperfield swiveled his head, eyes wide. "Who's your decorator? Looks like a Gestapo dungeon in a Paul Muni movie."

"Thank you," Kiet said.

"Okay, what's it gonna be? Bamboo shoots under the fingernails?"

"No," Binh said. "That's an obsolete Chinese method. We can do better."

"Terrific. Gonna wire my family jewels to the wall socket?"

"Good idea," Binh said, nodding in appreciation.

"Hey!"

Kiet said, "Mr. Chipperfield, you fibbed to us."

"Uh, how so?"

"You did not inform us that Tui Nha came to your hotel room."

Chipperfield hunched his shoulders and grinned. "Hey, c'mon. I didn't lie. I just forgot."

"What did he want?"

"To buy the heavyweight goodie."

"On his own behalf?"

"Damned if I know."

Kiet looked at Binh.

Binh asked, "The polygraph or the cattle prod or the tweezers?"

"Yes," Kiet said.

"Okay, fine. He was doing the inscrutable bit, but you don't have to be a rocket scientist to figure it was Fop Tia. They're buddy-buddy, you know."

"And your response was?"

"I told him to go take a flying fuck at a rolling doughnut. Numero uno, I don't have it. Numero two-oh, if I knew who did, I'd rat him out to you in a minute, Kiet. I know what that doodad means to Luong. It'd be like ripping off the Shroud of Turin. I might have what you call your basic situational ethics, but I'm not a total slime. When it comes to sacrilegious, Chick Chipperfield draws the line."

Kiet inhaled air into the floor of his chest. The nausea

created by Chipperfield's expression of provisional integrity passed. "Who has it?"

Chipperfield moved his head like a metronome. "That's the sixty-four-zillion-dollar question, big fella. Sorry."

"Very well."

Chipperfield brightened. "Does that mean you believe me?"

"Perhaps."

Chipperfield hopped off the stool and clapped his hands. "Great! When do I check out of Devil's Island?"

"You will remain in protective custody. We can't have the communists assassinating you."

"Commies? C'mon, Kiet. You know I was jerking your chain. Ridsa whacked out Al. Gimme an armed escort to the airport. I'll beeline it to Singapore. Ridsa and Tia, they won't have a clue where I am."

"No, not yet. You are potentially a—what is the applicable term, Captain?"

"Material witness."

"Splendid," Kiet said.

"Jesus! To what?"

"Directly or peripherally, to the entire mess. Nobody involved departs Hickorn until it is resolved."

Chipperfield stared at Kiet and saw a stone mask. There would be no room service and hostesses in his immediate future. "Man, if every gink who walked on my car lot and kicked a tire was like you, I'd've starved to death. Do something for me, will you? Move me to a different cell. Gimme some privacy. It's a goddamn zoo in there. We're packed cheek to jowl and nobody's ever heard of underarm deodorant. This one wacko, he has to take a leak, he gets up on a bench."

"In lieu of a balcony," Kiet said, thinking out loud. "Captain, arrange a transfer to nicer accommodations, please."

Binh said without enthusiasm that he would try and took

Chipperfield out. A few minutes later he returned, saying, "I reassigned him to a less crowded cell. Per your request."

"Good. Is he happy?"

"Happier, but something less than ecstatic," Binh said with a satisfied smile. "Only sixteen prisoners, Chipperfield included. The majority are vandals and drunks sleeping it off. No hardcore criminals, no head cases peeing on the floor. Superintendent, do you believe him?"

"I believe that Tui Nha went to Chipperfield as Fop Tia's agent. I believe that Ridsa has written Tia out of his scheme."

Binh nodded. "Yeah, me too. Ridsa's as ambitious and ruthless as they come. He probably gave Tia the cold shoulder. Whatever he's putting together with whom, he's shooting higher than Tia. And speaking of Ridsa, I'm heading out to check on my surveillance crew. Care to ride along?"

"No," Kiet said. "Progress beckons."

T h e r e was nobody inside UAT * CHANNEL 7-TV LUONG but Lin Aidit. She was stocking a display rack with maps and brochures. "Superintendent Kiet, thank goodness!"

Her eyes were red, colored by exhaustion and grief. Kiet asked, "Where are your clients?"

"I'm in a lull between tours. Later on, I'm conducting a downriver nature tour. If luck is with me, we'll see a tiger. I took this group to the National Assembly yesterday. One man described it as an aviary of loud, tame birds. Maybe I can provide a contrast of wild and stealthy creatures."

"I wish you that luck," Kiet said.

"Have you arrested Mr. Selkirk's murderer yet, Superintendent?"

"Alas, no."

"Mr. Chipperfield seems to have vanished. Is he in danger?"

"He is safe."

"That is a relief. I feel very, very guilty complaining about them to you the other day."

"Valid complaints," Kiet said. "How may I be of service?"

"I'll explain in the studio."

Studio? Kiet followed her into the back room, the heat chamber. He saw that one of the two carriage-mounted cameras was no longer decommissioned. It was in the center of the hellish room, its cord joined to the electronic control panels. A technician, wearing just shorts and sandals, sweating like a coolie, was squinting into the camera eyepiece, turning knobs, making adjustments. The camera lens was aimed at a table and chair. Nailed to the wall behind the chair was a white bedsheet.

"You are observing my problem, Superintendent."

"Excuse me?"

"Ambassador Smithson, the American ambassador, do you know him well?"

"I do," Kiet said. "I certainly do."

"He is very, very influential."

"Oh, yes," Kiet said.

"He is requesting a funeral ceremony for Mr. Selkirk. I have been ordered by associate deputy assistant ministers from Tourism, Foreign, and Internal Affairs to prepare for a news telecast. Ambassador Smithson is to deliver the eulogy himself. He says that Selkirk was killed by the Rouge. Is this so, Superintendent? Did the communists murder him?"

Kiet groaned.

"When the body is released by your police department, I'm instructed to notify the U.S. embassy. They requested a live telecast at the airport when Mr. Selkirk is placed on an airplane home, but we can't do that. Our cords aren't long enough and we don't have microwaves and satellite feeds and those things. I had to remind them that our equipment was manufactured a third of a century ago. So the ambas-

145

sador will deliver his eulogy in our studio with Mr. Selkirk's open coffin."

Where was Selkirk's body? Kiet wondered. Hickorn had no police morgue. They contracted with local mortuaries. But which one? He said, "We can't release the remains until the autopsy."

"When is the autopsy, Superintendent?"

Despite Binh's infatuation with District of Columbia–style forensic medicine, an autopsy had not been contemplated. The victim's skull had been bashed in with a Buddha. Ambulance Al had not accidentally toppled the Buddha off its stand onto his cranium. He had not lunged at it hara-kiri style. Kiet said, "I'll let you know."

"Then you can supply security? That was my primary question."

"Of course."

"I almost forgot. A sidewalk beggar inquired for you." Lin touched her nose. "He is terribly disfigured."

"Quoc," Kiet said. "Yes, I know him. What did he want?"

"He wouldn't say. He is afraid he will be harassed or detained if he goes to police headquarters."

"That is an unfortunate possibility."

"He knew you had been here. He asked me to relay his request when I next saw you."

"Thank you."

"Forgive my pushiness, Superintendent, but could you give me the approximate date when the autopsy will be finished? Those glorified clerks are hounding me."

As far as Kiet was concerned, Smithson and his ghoulish propaganda pageant could wait until the sun went into nova. He said, "Please convey to them what I plan to, that police science cannot be hurried."

I n t e r s p e r s e d in Captain Binh's breezy Westernisms was the random bromide. Kiet despised the bromides, homilies, and aphorisms of all cultures. No matter what language they were uttered in, they translated into Luongan too freely, and vice versa. They were the universal language of the lobotomized.

A Man's Home Is His Castle.

That evening, in his villa, the words looped inside Kiet's head. It was the variation that depressed him. Sun down, television on, Golden Tiger in hand, shutters latched, curtains drawn (he would not answer the door for Mai Le Trung or anyone else), he was hearing: A Man's Home Is His Enclave. A banality had become a temporary retreat from reality. In the morning he would have to open the gates of the stockade and duck arrows and tomahawks. But that was in the faraway future, eight hours from now. The moment belonged to "Gunsmoke," to an uplifting injection of Dillonism.

Tonight, Matt confronted a lynch mob, a necktie party. Their quarry, an innocent man, was atop a horse. Their rope was cinched to a tree limb, the noose set. Matt rode up with only seconds to spare. He quelled the mob with strong words of reason and a rifle butt to the snout of the mob leader, who incidentally proved to be the actual killer of the schoolmarm.

So there it was. Justice dispensed with a blend of verbal persuasion and physical violence. A balance of opposing forces was achieved. Yin and yang. So easy, so elemental.

Kiet shook his head in admiration. The man was not even Asian.

19

Bamsan Kiet awoke to Savhanakip Penulti-
mate, a Friday, a day of feasting and fellowship, a day
traditionally reserved for friendship, family, and food.
Festivities were usually conducted indoors and in large
groups. People who did not often see one another gathered
and renewed their bonds. A quietude, an uncommon seren-
ity fell over the Kingdom of Luong on Savhanakip Penultimate. It reminded Kiet of Christmas Eve. It was the day
before Savhanakip; from his perspective it was the eye of
the typhoon.

One gathering transcended ordinary fellowship. Savhanakip Penultimate was the date of His Royal Highness'
annual reception for senior Luongan governmental leaders
and foreign diplomats. A sumptuous buffet in the Royal
Palace ballroom ran from luncheon hour through dinner-
time.

Kiet too received an invitation. He chose not to attend,
not as a guest. He was too ashamed. There would be the
inevitable questions regarding the Golden Peacock rumor.
He knew he could not carry off his lie in such a stately

environment to a multitude of clever people. There he would be, Hickorn's ranking policeman, unconvincingly denying the existence of a crime he had failed to solve. Not the least of his fears was a calamitous loss of face.

Instead, he supervised security outside the Royal Palace, available to reconcile squabbles his starched and polished guards could not. There were the perennial gate crashers, social-climbing embassy flunkies without credentials. Their stories never deviated; they had forgotten to bring their invitations. Kiet sympathized and accompanied them back to their taxis and pedicabs.

To invited guests who arrived too early or too late, Kiet politely pointed out the calligraphed time ranges on their invitations. Since 1981 the reception had been loosely split into two shifts. The announced reason was that it had outgrown the ballroom. This was a fraction of the truth. The real reason was politics.

In 1981, the Bulgarian chargé d'affaires, an evangelical Stalinist, and a young American attaché, heady with the Cold War swagger of the newly elected U.S. president, mingled for a moment too long. The result was ideological nitroglycerin. Some gave the American the early advantage. He was lean and nimble, an accomplished tennis player. He landed skillful and solid punches, but the blows failed to drop the Bulgarian, a squat and immensely strong man whose musculature had developed during his early years on a collective farm. The Bulgarian just kept coming, muttering Slavic curses, ignoring the punishment. The onlookers who finally stepped in and peeled the Stalinist's stubby, calloused fingers from the semiconscious Cold Warrior's neck said later that Luong was sixty seconds from its Murder of the Century.

This year, the communist bloc was received first, the capitalists after a safe interim. Neutralists came and went as they pleased, and remained as long as they liked, which was customarily from beginning to end. Often inebriated and represented in large numbers because of the free food and drink, they tended to interject themselves into conversations, forming apolitical and obnoxious buffers between antagonists.

Today proceeded almost too smoothly. Hardly anyone was unauthorized or untimely. The conduct of His Royal Highness' guests was faultless to the point of soporific. Kiet's watch hands moved as if they were cast lead.

The arrival of Ambassador Dang and Madame Mai Le Trung was a rare pulse-quickener. Kiet and the Vietnamese exchanged greetings and smiles. Mai's smile and hello-how-are-you were too radiant, too convivial, bleached of any intimacy. Kiet watched as they walked toward the Royal Palace, close to each other and in lockstep. Their forearms once brushed. He had the queasy feeling that they were companions rather than colleagues. A couple.

When the sun had settled so low in the western sky that Kiet had to shade his eyes to look in that direction, the reception began to break up. The palace doors opened for Phorn Ridsa, then for Ambassador Smithson and his retinue.

Not now, he thought. If Ridsa or Smithson saw him and engaged him in conversation, he would be forced to listen to complaints and free advice. No, thank you. Kiet edged backward into the fringe of guests who were idling outside, chatting.

He had the sensation of being stared at, the peculiar clairvoyant feeling that everyone experiences and nobody can explain of eyes burning through the back of one's head. He turned around and faced a park, one of two separated by Mu Savhana on the north side of Avenue Leonid Brezhnev. The horizontal sun distributed long shadows from the trees and flowering shrubs. Kiet blinked and squinted, adjusting his vision to the strips of light and shade. Squatting on a snaking footpath, staring steadily at him, was Quoc, the leprous beggar with no nose.

Kiet had completely forgotten about the poor devil's visit to Lin Aidit. Quoc seemed to be lurking, poised to panhandle reception guests. Kiet approached him unsmiling, a policemen armed with admonitions. When he stood above Quoc, he knew he was wrong. There was no paper cup, no hat.

The beggar sprang to his feet, grinning obsequiously. He bowed and said, "Superintendent, sir, at last we are in contact."

Quoc's words were distorted by his impediment, but Kiet understood them. "What is it you need, Quoc?"

"It is what you may need, sir. It is what I saw yesterday."

"You could have gotten the information to me yesterday if you had gone to Headquarters."

"Oh no, sir. I could not. Confucius had a saying. He said that the essence of gentlemen is wind. The essence of small people is grass. The wind will blow over the grass and the grass must bend. I am the grass, the smallest of small people. Your policemen do not like—" Quoc passed a bony hand in front of his face. "—do not like any beggars and they hate beggars who look like me. They resent my very being."

"Perhaps," Kiet conceded. "What is your information?"

"I am invisible to people, sir. Did you realize that? I cannot smell, I cannot talk plainly, and I am old. People think I am deaf and mute too. At least they act like they do. They speak and they do things they would not dare do in the presence of a whole man."

Quoc paused, his face locked in an embittered contortion. Kiet suppressed his impatience and said nothing.

The beggar continued, "I beg at places where I am seen by people with extra money, sir. You condone me to and I am grateful. These people know much. You are my only friend, sir. Your recent adversities flood me with sorrow."

"Rumors," Kiet said.

"Rumors and reality," Quoc said. "In Hickorn, they are Siamese twins."

Kiet had never before talked at length with Quoc. The beggar's articulateness surprised Kiet and he told him so.

Quoc's grin returned. He tapped his temple and said, "The nuns at the leprosarium educated us well. They taught us that if we were to have any chance we had to learn hungrily and that while the germs eat our skin, they do not eat our brains."

"I am listening," Kiet said.

"Minister of Tourism Phorn Ridsa is a scoundrel. Do you share my hateful judgment, sir?"

Evasiveness and coyness would be insulting, Kiet thought. "Yes. Absolutely."

"There is gossip concerning the National Museum, sir."

"Yes."

"Gossip that does not necessitate repeating?"

"Thank you."

"Minister Ridsa came to the Postal Office yesterday morning, sir. I was on the steps passively seeking charity, as I was when you harkened to me from your automobile several days ago. Minister Ridsa parked his automobile on the street but he did not expeditiously disembark. He acted like he was waiting for somebody. He was noticeably nervous. Upon the passage of ten or fifteen minutes he got out. I comprehended that he wasn't waiting for anybody. Contrariwise, he was waiting for the Postal Office to be free of patrons. It was he and I alone on the steps and he did not afford me even a modest nuance of a glance."

Quoc hesitated, to lick dry, cracked lips. Kiet regretted his articulateness compliment. Quoc was exhibiting his vocabulary as if it were a photographic album of grand-children. The bulk of adjectives and adverbs might delay the story's conclusion past Savhanakip.

"He ambulated to the main doors cradling a package I ocularly evaluated as weighty and fragile."

153

"Ah," Kiet said. "How big a package?"

"Approximately a cubic foot. The main doors were not his means of ingress, however. He tergiversated."

"Excuse me."

Kiet's gruff tone informed Quoc that class was dismissed. "So sorry, sir. He changed his mind. He went down the steps and into the passageway by the building. He was skulking. A skulking gentlemen. A delightful sight! He knocked on a passageway door reserved for postal workers. He gave the employee who answered his parcel and some money."

"How much money?"

"Currency as thick as a slice of bread. Enough to mail the parcel to the moon."

"Superintendent!"

"Captain," Kiet said to Binh.

"I asked where you were. A guard saw you go into this park."

Kiet withdrew his wallet and gave Quoc a five-hundred zin note. He took the bill, touched fingers to his nose plug in prayer fashion, and squatted. The appearance of an armed policeman had broken the spell.

The disapproving Binh pointed downward and said, "Superintendent, five hundred—"

Kiet clasped Binh's arm, saluted Quoc, and escorted his adjutant out of the park. "You're too generous, Superintendent, too softhearted, too easy a mark."

"Not a gift. Wisely invested money," Kiet said. "I was paying an informant."

Binh rolled his eyes. "Him? What could he know?"

"The secrets of the universe."

"Huh?"

"In due time. But first, a report on the surveillance of Ridsa, please."

"I came to debrief my crew. Ridsa was at the reception.

154

They were standing by. He just left and they've picked him up again."

"I know he just left," Kiet said. "What do they have?"

"Same-o, same-o. Zilch."

"Their surveillance has been uninterrupted?"

"Well, yeah, except for about half to three-quarters of an hour yesterday."

"Immediately following our conference with him?"

"Yeah, how'd you know? They were watching the old embassy and his car, a green Mercedes. From out of nowhere, he drove up in another car. Somehow he ducked out on them. I guess you lit a fire under him."

"What are you driving?"

"A motorbike," Binh said.

Kiet gave him the keys to the Citroën. "Walk faster. It's on the next block."

"Where are we going?"

"The Postal Office."

"If it's superurgent, Superintendent, we'll make better time in the Honda. Traffic's no sweat. I can motor that little puppy through an eye of a needle."

Kiet had accelerated the pace to a jog. "Leave that trick to camels, Captain. I am too young to join my ancestors."

B i n h drove. Kiet narrated his discussion with Quoc, editing out the esoteric modifiers.

"Wow!" Binh said. "You *really* lit a fire under Ridsa. He figured Tia knew where he'd hidden the Peacock and went for it. He sure as hell hadn't clued Tia in, but he couldn't be sure Tia hadn't made a lucky guess, them being longtime buddies."

"Agreed."

"Ridsa moved it to the Postal Office. He'd probably planned to mail it all along, but thanks to your scam he jumped the gun."

"Yes."

"Where? To whom?"

Kiet's shrug became an involuntary wince. Binh had expertly avoided a pedicab that had crossed in front of them, reacting, of course, with gas pedal and steering wheel rather than brakes. Kiet saw in order: a blur, the pedicab's tire-tread pattern, the frayed shorts of its operator.

"Superintendent?"

"I don't know, although we can probably assume he's posting it out of Luong."

"Will it still be there? Parcels and letters have been known to disappear into the core of the earth after they're mailed, but if that leper fed you the straight dope, Ridsa paid for preferential treatment."

"He may not have been buying efficiency. He may have been buying confidentiality. Your men at Hickorn International?"

"Good point, Superintendent. They're on the ball. Overseas mail bins are of uppermost priority. No way it'll skate by them."

As Phorn Ridsa had for thirty to forty-five minutes? Kiet thought testily as the Postal Office came into view. Binh stopped the Citroën in the middle of the street. They ran to the doors and shook them. Locked. Signs printed in Luongan, French, and English proclaimed: CLOSED. HOURS 9–11, 3–5.

Kiet looked at his watch. 5:01. The door pulls were massive brass, smooth curves topped by gargoyles, a colonial French architect's ideal of beauty. Binh was rattling them back and forth, making an awful racket. "They're in there, the lazy bastards," he said.

Through soiled windows Kiet saw dim light and movement.

"The night shift, sorting mail," Binh said.

"Are they wearing earplugs?"

"It's the same in American post offices, Superintendent.

156

One second before or after customer hours and it's like they're hermetically sealed."

"Suggestions on getting in, please."

Binh unsnapped his holster. "We're talking about a national emergency. I'll blast the locks."

Matt would do that, Kiet thought, but Matt was not keeping the peace in Hickorn the day before Savhanakip. "No. The noise would attract an audience."

"Yeah, you're right." Binh snapped his fingers. "Wait a second, I know a postal supervisor. I'll go to his home. He'll let us in and keep his mouth shut too."

Kiet suggested assigning an officer to ensure that no mail was removed from the Postal Office in the meantime; he would prefer to do it himself, but a loitering superintendent of police might be a bit conspicuous. Binh said he'd detail an officer and stop at Kiet's villa with the postal supervisor. Kiet said splendid—going in after dark is better anyhow—and told Binh to use the Citroën.

He rode a taxi home, thinking en route how the mess was almost over, how all might yet be well.

It would not be the first time he had been wrong that day.

20

''Kiet.''

Kiet flinched and turned.

Mai Le Trung was standing a meter behind him. "I'm sorry I startled you."

"No. You didn't," Kiet lied. He had been unlatching the gate to his villa and there she was. The woman had a knack of materializing, like a wraith.

"I've been waiting. It is imperative that we talk."

When isn't it imperative? he almost asked. He escorted her into his home, wondering *what now?* If she had in mind a heavy-breathing tumble between the sheets and a subsequent search of his clothing, she was in for a disappointment. The Vietnamese beauty's treachery had deadened his loins.

He did not invite her to sit, he did not offer her a refreshment. He looked at her and coolly said, "Very well. Talk."

"You are angry with me, my lover. What have I done?"

Her little girl's petulance was not becoming. A Marxist guerrilla-spy *pouting*? No, thank you. It did not ring true.

Kiet looked at his watch and said, "I am not angry, Madame. I am merely strapped for time."

She exhaled a weak, resigned sigh—passion was not to be an ally tonight—and said, "We have uncovered a plot. Luongan army officers are planning to assassinate members of our soccer team."

"What members?"

"Any and all they can."

"When?"

"During the parade tomorrow."

"How did you uncover the plot?"

"I am not at liberty to reveal sources, Kiet, but I know it's true."

"What army officers."

"Your high command in Obon is instigating a coup d'état."

Kiet paused to analyze this outrageous accusation. Obon, Luong's only other city of note, was located in the northern highlands, 175 kilometers from Hickorn. It was the headquarters of the Royal Luongan Army's Second Military District, whose nominal mission was neutralization of the Luong Rouge.

Since Rouge attacks were pitifully spasmodic and ineffectual, Second District was able to devote steadfast attention to a paramilitary project: the opium trade. Luong's mountainous frontier skirted a point on the Golden Triangle. Troops bought, sold, and transported the raw gum.

Obon had forever been a fascist fiefdom ruled by the army. Their leaders were ambitious and corrupt, yes, but Kiet could not picture a cabal of generals and colonels concocting a Hickorn bloodbath. A coup? No. The chaos would be bad for business.

"They kill your players and take over our country? Excuse me, Madame, but I don't fathom your logic."

"It is more complicated. They have the Golden Peacock."

"Excuse me?" Kiet said innocently.

"Your national treasure that has been stolen."

By reflex, Kiet nearly denied the theft. "What do they intend to do with it?"

"We aren't certain, but we think they're going to announce that Prince Pakse sent it to France, where he will soon follow to live in exile, whiling away his final years with billiard playing and high living."

Cynics asserted that His Royal Highness was already in exile. They did not say it in the company of Bamsan Kiet. "He enjoys great wealth in Hickorn, Madame."

"He has duties and ceremonies to perform, a decorum to maintain," Mai said. "He cannot enjoy his riches as decadently as he—"

Kiet was glaring hard at her. She noticed, pursed her lips, and resumed. "Mm—I mean that is how the rebel officers will justify themselves."

Kiet closed his eyes. A hard-edged puzzle piece floated into the void. Then another. And another. And another. And another. The pieces were as bright and sticky as a summer noon. They docked perfectly, sealing out every seam of darkness. The puzzle was his Peacock–Doublemint Twins–Ridsa mess. The puzzle was solved. Thanks to Madame Mai's haltingly spoken sentence, each recalcitrant puzzle part had suddenly become magnetized, irresistibly drawn to the others. *Solved.*

"When, please?"

"Our intelligence sources believe the announcement will coincide with the assassinations. Agents are situated to seize Hickorn's radio stations."

"Agents?"

"Hickorn-based soldiers who are accomplices with the Obon officers."

"I see. Then?"

"A convoy from Obon will roll into Hickorn to restore order and arrest Pakse. They will invade with all the force they can muster. The assassinations will be attributed to

161

Pakse loyalists who commit them so he can escape in the confusion. Hickorn barracks units will be caught off guard and isolated with roadblocks. They will either be forced to surrender and cooperate in the coup or be slaughtered if they attempt to resist."

Crazy, Kiet thought. Lunacy. But fascinating lunacy. "A military dictatorship. The end of the kingdom," he said with a fabricated frown.

"The Socialist Republic of Vietnam and the Kingdom of Luong are friends, Kiet. Though our politics differ, we respect your independence and autonomy. Your status quo is vital to the stability of Southeast Asia."

"It is?"

Mai nodded. "It is. A military government is not in anyone's best interest. Interference by foreign powers would inevitably ensue. The Americans and Russians and Chinese have coveted Luong for decades."

Kiet returned the nod, thinking that she had conveniently excluded the Vietnamese.

"The southern sector of our homeland in the 1960s and 1970s is an instructional model, a testament to the horrors of a venal army dictatorship. The Saigon puppets and their imperialist running dog—"

"Saigon," Kiet interrupted. "You said Saigon, not Ho Chi Minh City."

Mai flushed. "I was speaking in historical perspective."

"Of course," Kiet said, subduing a smile. Political zealots were so easily goaded. You could count on them for a moment of fun in the ugliest of circumstances.

"Ambassador Dang asked me to seek help from you, Kiet."

"Why me?"

"Our foreign ministry has forbidden us to interfere in Luongan internal affairs. The policy is correct but we feel an obligation to prevent this tragedy if at all possible."

"Why me?"

162

"We are new in Luong. We have not made many binding friendships yet. Ambassador Dang and I asked ourselves whom we knew and respected, whom we knew to be a patriotic royalist, who was important enough to deter stupid, reckless people."

"Ah. Me."

"You, Kiet."

"Prostrating myself in the path of a tank," Kiet said dreamily. "I don't know. We Luongans are not fond of martyrdom."

"Deter, I said. Not die. Dissuade them. And may I suggest that you remember your pledge to protect our soccer players. You are being cold and sarcastic to me, Kiet. You loved me while you were between my legs."

Her renewed pout was erotic, rather exciting. Perhaps it was that or perhaps it was her reference to sexual mechanics. Whichever, Madame Mai's antennae had received the signal. She was touching his sides ever so lightly, saying, "Will you?"

"Of course," he said raspingly, the crack in his voice not entirely theatrical.

"What will you do?"

What-will-you-do. A monotone cadence. A teacher prodding the correct answer from a student's mouth. "Well, the Obon warlords and I have met casually while they've been in Hickorn. It was a strain for me to be cordial, but I am willing to talk to them. I cannot contest them with men and guns, and if Hickorn troops are, as you say, in on the plot, I would not know whom to confide in here."

"We think alike, Kiet," Mai said with a thin smile that appeared to be one of relief. "It would be easier, though, if you liked them and they liked you. They would be more apt to listen."

I am expected to disagree, Kiet deduced. "I disagree, Mai. A friend is readily bribed or coerced. You know him.

You know if his greed or submission is genuine. No, I prefer to be unpredictable."

"All right, you make good sense. What will you say?"

What-will-you-say. "I don't know. Perhaps an appeal to their patriotism. Perhaps a ruse. The military in Hickorn is on to them and prepared to destroy their convoy, and so forth. Perhaps I can sell myself as a deal-making emissary. They love money above all. I'll think of something. If I can reach Obon tonight."

"I recall that Royal Air Luong's Obon shuttle makes three trips daily. The last flight leaves in ninety minutes."

Kiet eased backward. "Splendid. Luck is with us. I'll go at once to the air—"

Mai moved forward. "No, there is time. Time for love."

Kiet heard popping sounds.

"Savhanakip firecrackers," Mai said.

The small explosions grew louder, closer. Mai was kissing him, her tongue searching, her pelvis grinding.

"*Ummppht*," Kiet said, responding.

"Superintendent!"

Captain Binh blocked the doorway. His backdrop was a mist of foul blue smoke. Binh's mouth was agape in profound disgust. Kiet imagined an eighteenth-century French Catholic missionary surprising an up-country Luongan tribesman in the act of worshipping cattle entrails.

Kiet and Mai separated. Mai folded her arms and looked at a wall. Kiet smiled sheepishly. Kiet's cat walked in from the kitchen and yawned.

"Superintendent, the postal—"

"Never mind about the letter I asked you to mail. Drive me to Hickorn International."

"Huh?"

Kiet swished his hands, as if sweeping dust. "Go. I have to be in Obon."

"Huh?"

164

The cat was rubbing against Mai's legs. "Please feed him," Kiet said.

Mai's eyes were more feline than the wretched animal's. Feral eyes. She blew him a kiss.

Outside, the blue mist was a suffocating fog. Kiet coughed and said, "Is this the Los Francisco smog you've told me about? Where did it come from?"

"Los Angeles, not San Francisco."

"Yes. San Angeles," Kiet said, hacking. "What?"

Binh pointed across the street to the origin of the weather inversion, to opaque smoke wafting from under the Citroën's hood. "The engine blew a block from your villa, Superintendent. I nursed it the rest of the way. I don't get it. That car ran like a top."

A top routinely spun at thirty miles per hour in low gear, Kiet thought. Weeping from the airborne poison and partially blind, he stumbled into the prow of Chipperfield's Chrysler Imperial. "Old Yellow is our substitute transportation," he said.

Binh was game. He eased out of Kiet's courtyard, tramped on the gas pedal, burning tire rubber, and hurtled westbound on Avenue Che Guevara. The turnoff to Richard Nixon Boulevard and Hickorn International Airport approached alarmingly fast. "Is this Obon stuff for real, Superintendent?"

"No, but pretend for two or three streets in case she is watching. And slow down, *please*. I have no intention of meeting my ancestors while skewered by a lamppost."

The sensitive Binh was offended. He expressed his umbrage by decelerating to a crawl. He used the automobile's turn signal lever and exercised excruciating caution before changing lanes or direction. The abnormal time required to travel three blocks north on Nixon, two blocks west on Avenue Margaret Thatcher, and two backtracking blocks south on Rue Ho Chi Minh was sufficient for Kiet to relate Madame Mai's story.

165

"That's goofy, Superintendent, totally off the wall."

"Agreed, but might I have missed a rumor?"

"You know better than I that Luongan coups self-destruct. Nobody can keep their yap buttoned. You couldn't sneak a slingshot into Hickorn without somebody bragging it up in a bar, trying to score on a babe. Second District moving on us en masse? That's one hundred percent, USDA prime bullshit. A scam on that scale would be as subtle as a turd in a punch bowl."

Laced in Binh's bathroom slang were clues that he also doubted Madame Mai's tale. Kiet said, "You have a Westernism, a term for the hunting of unattainable birds."

"Wild-goose chase."

"Yes."

"She's sending you on one, Superintendent. She's smooth talking you out of town. How come?"

"Excellent question," Kiet said.

"Uh, on the subject of, you know, her, Superintendent . . ."

Kiet suppressed a groan. Here it comes. A lecture. The lad was going to treat him to son-to-father wisdom.

"She is a dedicated communist. During the American war, she fought with the Vietcong."

"I know her background," Kiet said patiently.

"She is incredibly gorgeous."

"Yes."

"I've heard stories of how the most beauteous Vietcong women served their cause. These stories are bizarre and horrifying but they've been verified, Superintendent."

"Go on, Captain. Please do not deprive me."

"Well, they'd, you know, insert razor blades and seduce GIs."

Kiet's manhood shrank and shriveled, as if his undershorts had been packed with ice. "Interesting."

"Now I'm not suggesting anything that blatant."

"Thank you."

"I'm just saying how their minds work. The end justifies the means, et cetera."

"We are not at war with Vietnam," Kiet said.

Binh did not seem to hear. He said, "Disease was another method. They did that too. You wouldn't find out for a couple of weeks. By then, the girl was long gone. Disease was smarter than razor blades. She filets your meat, you're going to be upset. If you still can, you're going to give her a bad day too."

"Understandably so," Kiet said. "Diseases?"

"Venereal diseases."

"Oh? Not measles?"

Kiet's humorless humor missed its mark. "They have these new strains going around, Superintendent. AIDS and everything. Your pecker rots off and you die. Penicillin hasn't got a prayer."

"I appreciate your hyperbole and your concern," Kiet said. "Take the next left, please."

"By the way, where are we going?"

"The Postal Office. By the way, where is the postal supervisor you retrieved?"

Binh gritted his teeth. "The bastard, did I say he was a friend?"

Kiet shrugged.

"He was throughout school. We played soccer and drank and chased skirts. But that's *fini*. I told him we needed in and told him I couldn't tell him why we needed in. He gave me this form to fill out in quadruplicate. I fill it out and he'll give it to *his* supervisor first thing Monday morning for approval. They're closed Savhanakip and Sunday. I said we had to get in now. He said we couldn't get in after hours unless the forms were completed and that he couldn't get his boss' okay until Monday morning. I asked him what the hell good was an after-hours authorization form if it didn't get the place unlocked for us after hours. He said that with a properly signed authorization Monday morning we could get in after hours Monday night. His postal service career has made a donkey out of him, Superintendent."

Binh spread a thumb and index finger an eighth of an inch apart. "I was this close to drawing my weapon and abducting him, him and his door keys."

"I applaud your restraint, Captain."

"Yeah. Like you said, we don't want to attract an audience. Me booting his slimy bureaucratic butt up the Postal Office steps sure as hell would."

Kiet fixed a Dillonesque stare on the windshield and jabbed both forefingers. "We will deal with the problem of an audience as it arises. We no longer have time for niceties. Go."

Binh smiled gleefully. "Right on, Superintendent!"

He depressed the accelerator, throwing Kiet back in his seat.

21

The pseudo-Grecian facade of the Postal Office was illuminated by a half-moon and by street lamps, fifty percent of which were in working order. Its neighbors were government subministries and wholesale merchants whose hours were equally rigid. Save for the occasional taxi or bicyclist nobody was in the area.

Binh got out of the car. The uniformed officer assigned to watch the Postal Office quickstepped to him and saluted. After a short conference, Binh told Kiet, "No one has gone in or out."

Kiet got out of the car too and gazed placidly at the ponderous stone building. Madame Mai's unknowing disclosure had made him confident to the verge of arrogance. *Solved.* He felt giddy, almost light on his feet.

"Superintendent, shall I release my man?"

"No," Kiet said, walking up the steps. "If we are excessively noisy, we may need a spokesman to lie for us."

They peered through the grimy windows and saw dim light and blurred movement.

"Same-o, same-o," Binh said. "What do we do?"

Kiet gestured to the doors. "Initially, a civilized overture."

Binh rapped hard and waited. He then grasped the brass gargoyles in a stranglehold and rocked them until Kiet's sinuses vibrated. Binh cursed, kicked solid brass, and wiped perspiration from his brow. "Superintendent, we'd have better luck raising the dead."

"Shoot off the lock, please."

Binh beamed. "I thought you'd never ask."

"The windows are barred on the inside and as you previously stated, this is a national emergency."

Binh's Colt .45 automatic was out of his patent leather holster and cocked in one smooth slap. Kiet had had no idea. He wondered if the lad practiced before a mirror. He visualized him in Dodge City, a high-quality sidekick replacement for the gimpy Chester. In fast-draw show-downs Binh and Matt would be an invincible duo.

"Stand clear of ricochets, Superintendent."

Kiet backed away and plugged his ears with his pinkies. Binh fired and fired, expending his clip. Sparks glinted. His aim was accurate. The lockset and surrounding metal were thoroughly dented and perforated.

Binh held the weapon to his lips and with panache blew smoke from the barrel. He twirled the Colt by its trigger guard, reholstered, and tested the doors. They did not budge, did not rattle in their sashes, let alone open. Ruptured metal had jammed the innards.

"Old-world craftsmanship," Binh said in disgust. "This has to be the one thing those old Frogs did right."

"Perhaps they heard and will let us in."

Binh wiped a pane with his sleeve, squinted, and said, "No chance. They probably think it was firecrackers. What's Plan B, Superintendent?"

Kiet scuffed his feet on the top step. It was smooth, wide, and shallow. He counted one, two, three; only three puny steps separated the sidewalk from the entrance. He went to the Chrysler, paced off its width, returned to the Postal Office doors, and paced off their width.

"How would you gauge it, Captain? I'd guess that Old Yellow is narrow enough and amply powered for the task."

Binh sighed sadly. "A damned shame. This baby is a classic."

"National emergency," Kiet reminded him.

"What the hell, let's go for it. I once went to a demolition derby in America."

"Excuse me?"

Binh smiled. "Yeah, you take a bunch of beater cars to a field or a stadium and smash them into each other. The last car moving wins."

"Insane," Kiet said.

"Fender-bender City. Great fun." Binh was behind the wheel, revving the engine.

"No."

"I'll buckle up, Superintendent. I'll be okay."

"My adjutant an automotive kamikaze? No, thank you. Out."

"Aw."

"Find us a heavy object. We shall contrive a guided missile."

Binh removed the car's jack from the trunk. Kiet positioned Old Yellow perpendicular to the Postal Office, abutting the opposite curb. He straightened the front tires, secured the seat belt around the steering wheel, and laid the jack on the accelerator.

"I'll take over, Superintendent," Binh yelled. "Our missile launch is gonna be hairy. No aspersion intended."

Kiet was to a small degree offended, but he was not foolhardy. Old Yellow sounded like thunder. There were tasks for boys, there were tasks for men. Physical quickness was in the purview of the lithe and immature. He withdrew, no face lost.

Binh extended a hand into Old Yellow, punched the

dashboard transmission selector, and also withdrew, slipping on his trailing heel and falling backward into Kiet's arms.

Old Yellow pitched ahead, fishtailing. Kiet pivoted Binh out of reach of the rear bumper, a chromium meathook. The automobile thumped up the steps, undaunted by a blown left-front tire and disemboweled exhaust system. Enraged by its wounds, so it seemed to Kiet. A rabid steel elephant that sheared the majestic brass doors as if they were rice paper screens, penetrated to its windshield pillar, shuddered, wheezed, and died.

The uniformed patrolman had meanwhile retreated to an intersection after the gunfire began and had crept around the corner to smoke a cigarette when Hickorn's number one and number two law enforcement officers maneuvered that monster motorcar sideways. Deranged conduct terrified all cops, and top-level departmental strategy was none of his business anyway. The horrendous explosion of metal against metal had drawn him, sending him sprinting to the Postal Office, sickened by a sense of duty he could not overcome.

Captain Binh, whom he idolized, was on the roof of the monster motorcar, crouching, entering the maw it had created. Nearby was Superintendent Kiet, who upon seeing the patrolman, waved and motioned him to come. The patrolman admired Superintendent Kiet too, although Superintendent Kiet never wore a uniform and did not carry a gun.

"Sir?"

"A traffic accident," Kiet said. "The car's brakes and steering failed, and it careened into the Postal Office."

"It did?"

"No," Kiet said.

"Oh," said the officer, drawing the syllable out on rounded lips. "That is how I am to answer curious onlookers?"

"Please."

The patrolman saluted, did an about-face, and assumed a position of parade rest. The patrolman's brother repaired and sold bicycle tires and tubes from a pedal-powered cart. He was doing very well and had been urging the patrolman to join the business. The patrolman used this opportunity to reconsider the offer.

Kiet followed Binh into the Postal Office, nearly losing his footing on a marble floor made slick by fluids dripping from the maimed Chrysler. Customers were served at a wide counter in the narrow lobby. Mail was handled in the back. Binh was already there, hands on hips in an aggressive posture, facing three cowering clerks.

Kiet scanned the room, which occupied the remainder of the building. Letters and printed matter and parcels were piled haphazardly on shelves along the walls and on long rows of tables and bins. He supposed that there was a system to this clutter, but none was apparent.

"These guys are the night sorting crew, Superintendent," Binh said.

"Are they cooperating?"

"Nope. I didn't beat around the bush either. I asked them where the goody Minister Ridsa delivered was. They claim ignorance. They said to ask the day shift."

Kiet examined the room again. Thousands and thousands of packages. Those qualifying as Quoc's approximate cubic foot: hundreds and hundreds. He groaned. An interminable session of ripping paper and cutting twine awaited. Unless—

"There is no communication between you gentlemen and the day crew?"

The three clerks shook their heads.

"Innocents," Kiet said angrily. "Why is it that innocents are the ones to die?"

Binh looked at Kiet. The three clerks looked *intently* at Kiet.

"Alas," he said. "Maniacs and their stupid political crusades. They protest a regime by killing innocent people. What logic is there to that, Captain?"

"Uh, well," Binh said. "None."

"What time, Captain, did the caller say the bomb was set to explode?"

Binh caught on. He acknowledged the deception with a toothy grimace that camouflaged a grin, a jerky glance at his wristwatch, and a croaking, "My God, Superintendent! We've got under eighteen minutes!"

"I suppose we should evacuate the premises," Kiet said.

"Ten kilos of *plastique* will level the neighborhood," Binh said. "Shitstorm City."

"Not if we disarm it. You," he told one of the clerks, "bring a pail of water."

"I am not a brave man," the clerk stammered.

"Nor am I, but international terrorism cannot be condoned," Kiet said. "Where shall we begin the search?"

"There are so many packages," said another clerk.

"An impossibility," cried the third. "Eighteen minutes is not—"

"Seventeen going on sixteen," Binh said, monitoring his watch.

"You said we should evacuate, sir."

"I changed my mind. Nobody goes anywhere. I, for one, will gladly sacrifice my life to stymie these fiends. The five of us can—"

"My best friend works days," blurted the clerk who had been ordered to fetch water. "He gave special service to Minister Ridsa."

"Keep talking," Kiet said.

"Minister Ridsa paid him for precision routing."

"Excuse me?"

"Exact timing, sir. He paid airmail rates plus a personal bonus so that his mailing would be at the airport tomorrow morning. My friend was not conspiring to smuggle, sir. He

174

did not know the contents of the mailing. He did not know that Minister Ridsa was a communist terrorist."

Bribery to assure that a federal employee merely did his job was the Luongan trait that dispirited Kiet the most. It was the glue on an odious label: Third World. "And you are assisting your friend?"

"Yes sir."

"Is your friend paying you?"

The clerk lowered his head. "My friend is generous, sir."

"Where is our bomb, please?"

The clerk led Binh and Kiet to a steel-framed canvas pushcart. "He put it in with junk mail so it would not be lost."

"Junk mail?"

"Unsolicited advertising fliers, Superintendent," Binh explained. "The stuff gorges the United States postal service."

"We never saw junk mail until Unknown Asia Tours," said the clerk. "Now everybody in the world sends it to Hickorn. The junk mail is sorted last. My friend stashed it there so it wouldn't be disturbed tonight. He was instructed by Minister Ridsa to personally take it to the airport in the morning."

On top was a layer of identical envelopes. Kiet picked one out. It was plump and colorful, the addresser an American publishing house. Bold letters announced that YOU MAY HAVE ALREADY WON $1,000,000!!!! The addressee was a Hickorn resident named OCCUPANT. Kiet looked further. Different addresses, same name. Occupant. How could it be that such a common surname was unknown to him? Occupant did not even sound Luongan. It had a Laotian ring. And for what reason were million-dollar prizes being awarded to the Occupant clan?

Binh read Kiet's puzzlement and said, "It's a big come-on, Superintendent. I'll fill you in later."

175

"The bomb, sir," said the nervous and profusely perspiring clerk.

"Ten minutes," Binh said. "Nine-fifty-nine, fifty-eight, fifty-seven."

"Nine minutes!" the clerk wailed as he plunged his arms into the cart. Dog-paddling like a drowning swimmer, he flung out the million-dollar offerings.

"Eight minutes," Binh said.

"Already?" Kiet asked.

"I'm—I'm touching it." The clerk was panting, jack-knifed on the cart's rim, his feet dangling.

"Out," Kiet said, tapping his hip. "You've done nice work, but leave the rest to us. We do not want you triggering the detonator. Captain Binh is a trained bomb disposal expert."

"Sir, I beg you, may we go?"

"No. You and your colleagues hurry for the water. Each of you bring a bucket."

They scurried off for water. Binh lifted out the package and placed it on a bench. "Weighs a ton," he said, grunting.

"Gold does," Kiet said. "Let's have a look."

Binh carefully sliced into a corner with his pocketknife and peeled back corrugated cardboard and the outer wrapping, revealing a delicate, golden feather tip. They were for a moment overwhelmed by emotions they would never be able to articulate. Neither man had ever before laid hands on the Golden Peacock. Each did, ever so gingerly, ever so reverently.

Binh finally said, "The wrapping's stamped with the Royal seal."

"Easy enough to counterfeit," Keit said.

"It's addressed to a Ren Thap in Paris," Binh said. "Why is that name familiar?"

"His Royal Highness' dissolute nephew," Kiet said.

Binh snapped his fingers. "Yeah, right. He went off to school in France ten or twelve years ago. He was expelled in about five minutes, but stayed in Europe. A real party animal. He's wrecked a couple of Ferraris."

"And a Maserati."

"Three wives divorced him."

"Four," Kiet said.

"Wow!" Binh said. "The Peacock's dropped at the airport tomorrow, Savhanakip. It stands out like a sore thumb. Either my guys or customs seize it. Can you imagine the fireworks?"

"Indeed."

They heard a side door slam. Binh smirked. "I guess the boys are going to the Ma San River for our water. We'd best hustle the Peacock to the museum or the Royal Palace super fast."

"Agreed," Kiet said.

Binh scaled the Chrysler. Kiet transferred the Peacock to him and followed on an unsteady stairway of wrinkled chromium. In the street, lured by the break-in noise, was the inevitable audience. Kiet estimated fifty and increasing—pedestrians and a smattering of bicycles and pedicabs. He searched their eyes. No fear. Good. The water gatherers had undertaken their mission so conscientiously that they had neglected to warn their countrymen of the impending explosion.

People clustered around the patrolman-spokesman-designated liar. They were placid, happy, seemingly amused by the mechanical shortcomings of gargantuan Western automobiles. The officer reported to his superiors: "The crowd is satisfied by my explanations, gentlemen."

"Splendid. Please remain until they disperse."

The patrolman was staring at the box Captain Binh held like a newborn baby.

"Opium," Kiet said.

"Ten kilos worth," Binh said. "A big-league drug bust."

"Continue your fine work," Kiet said. "Tell the gallery about the narcotics if they inquire."

The officer's salute was limp, almost insubordinate, accompanied by a sigh. Kiet wondered what his problem was. He asked Binh, "Can Old Yellow be driven?"

"It's history, Superintendent."

"Mu Savhana is a long walk."

"Not to worry," Binh said.

22

Binh's not-to-worry solution to their transportation dilemma was a motorized pedicab, a cyclo dop. *Cyclo* was slang for the French words for "bicycle" and "tricycle." *Dop* was grammatical Luongan for "misadventure," specifically a violent mishap. Kiet savored the black humor ingrained in Hickornian argot, but not while he was seated in an object of it.

The cyclo dop was a three-wheeler with a popping, smoke-belching engine that ruptured eardrums and seared lungs. Passengers sat in front, providing shock absorption for the driver in event of collisions, which were frequent. The cyclo dop traded the relative safety and comfort of the taxicab for agility and a cheap fare. It was the transport mode of the pauper, the fool, the time-urgent.

Poor, foolish, and hurried, Kiet thought as the machine howled away from the Postal Office; we are at least two out of three. And how can you be anything but poor if you die?

"Look!" Binh yelled.

It seemed that their after-hours admittance to the Postal Office had awakened Hickorn. They were passing a disorderly array of foot traffic and vehicles, and Binh's exclamation had been directed at a green Mercedes-Benz sedan.

"Ridsa?" Kiet asked needlessly, twisting in his seat to see the Mercedes U-turn.

"Faster!" Binh screamed at the driver.

The bewildered driver looked back as the Mercedes skidded, reversed its path, and pursued. He stared straight ahead, pretending not to hear Binh.

Binh shook his fist at him. "This is official police business! Faster!"

The cyclo dop was slowing, not accelerating. Kiet understood the driver's reluctance to be the trophy of a wild chase, especially one in which the police, normally hunters, were the hunted. He probably had seven children and a yearly income that when converted to hard currency did not exceed four hundred U.S. dollars. He was not eager to orphan his children, nor to destroy the machine that earned him his money, not for something as abstract as good versus evil. It was simply none of his business.

The Mercedes was gaining ground. Kiet held up a thousand-zin note and moved his lips, forming, "Faster, please."

The driver snapped it out of his fingers and power surged from the tiny engine. The green Mercedes-Benz receded.

"Higher octane for his fuel tank," Kiet told Binh.

They were around the corner, eastbound on Avenue Alexandre Loubet, Kiet and Binh clutching the ballast between them, the Golden Peacock. The Mercedes sped north on Mu Luong. Binh said, "He had someone with him."

"Who?"

"Couldn't tell. Think we lost him?"

"No," Kiet said.

They crossed Rue Ho Chi Minh, and headed left, northward, on Mu Pakse. The Mercedes reappeared. It had taken the second cross street, Avenue Leonid Brezhnev, doubling back to cut them off.

"Jesus H. Christ," Binh said. "He's going to ram us head-on."

"Point your gun at them," Kiet ordered.

"It's empty."

"They don't know that."

"Oh, right," Binh said, quick-drawing. With a two-handed grip and a marksman's squint for effect, he took aim.

The Mercedes nosed downward as it braked. It swerved to its left, into an alley.

"Turn around," Kiet told the driver.

"No," Binh argued. "We're near the palace; it's only three more blocks to the museum."

"Look," Kiet said, pointing north. The grille of the Mercedes was just visible at Brezhnev, to their right. "They're waiting to squash us."

"My gun."

"Do you think they will believe that bluff again?"

Binh shook his head, saying, "Fool me once, shame on you. Fool me twice, shame on me."

"Whatever," Kiet said, twirling a finger over his head. "Driver, please go."

With hand signals, he spun around and sent the cyclo dop westbound on Loubet, then north on Ho Chi Minh. "They know where we want to go," Kiet said to Binh. "They have us blocked. If we take the short route, the last thing we shall see before our ancestors is the sedan's undercarriage."

"Okay," Binh said. "We'll make a long loop, eight or ten blocks, and hit Mu Savhana from the far end."

"Hopefully, unless we come upon a patrolman in the interim."

"With a loaded gun," Binh said.

"Yes."

"Don't hold your breath, Superintendent. Every man in the area is no doubt at the Postal Office. Say, we could—"

"Creep through that mob? No, thank you. Ridsa may have friends covering such a retreat."

"Yeah, right."

They crossed Avenue Leonid Brezhnev. The Mercedes turned. Kiet saw its rear tires spin, scorching rubber. It came toward Rue Ho Chi Minh.

"Eight blocks to go," Binh said. "They'll overtake us easily. Hey!"

"What?"

"The TV station," Binh cried. "I've got a brainstorm you'll love."

Kiet thought: UAT * CHANNEL 7-TV LUONG. A sanctuary? Why not? He signaled to the driver by thrusting his hand to the right. They swung into an alley on two wheels. Kiet held both hands up. The cyclo dop ground to a halt. The Mercedes raced northbound behind them. Kiet caught a glimpse of its passenger. A female. Beautiful. Vietnamese.

They jumped out and heard brakes screech. Kiet gave their trembling driver another thousand-zin note, advising him to head across Pakse into the park on the opposite side and hide. No further persuasion was necessary. The cyclo dop departed in a noxious cloud.

"You know, Superintendent, we could damn near sprint to the palace from here. It's like maybe a hundred meters to the gates."

"Sprint? With the sedan poised on Brezhnev or Savhana to pick us off?" Kiet said. "Undercarriage. Ancestors."

"All right," Binh conceded. "The station is kitty-corner. That idea is better anyway. Brilliant if I may say so."

"You may," Kiet said. "But will we be able to get in at this late hour? We have no Chrysler Imperial with which to pick their lock."

"It's prime time, Superintendent. They're telecasting. Somebody's got to be manning the store."

"Ah," Kiet remembered. "'Gunsmoke.'"

They looked both ways for oncoming traffic, particularly green automobiles sporting tri-star hood ornaments. None, nothing. Binh indeed sprinted, carrying the Golden Peacock, youthful legs pumping high. Kiet valiantly trailed him across the diagonal, into Unknown Asia Tours—Channel Seven, legs not pumping high.

"Superintendent Kiet," said Lin Aidit.

"Are you always on duty, Lin?" Kiet asked, gasping.

"What is the matter with your voice and your face, Superintendent?"

"My face?"

"You're crimson. Are you all right?"

"Yes. I was merely sprinting."

"Hello, Lin," Binh said, tipping his cap.

She ignored him and answered Kiet's question. "Yes, I know I'm working beyond my usual fourteen-hour day, but there are last-minute preparations I was commanded to make for tomorrow."

"My brainstorm—" Binh said to Kiet.

"Brain," Lin Aidit said to nobody. "He exposes his brain whenever he unzips his trousers."

"I've been enmeshed in important cases," Binh pleaded, tearing at the Golden Peacock's wrapping.

Enmeshed? "Please, Captain."

"Yes, sir. To the studio." Binh rushed behind the counter, discarding paper.

Kiet and Lin walked after him, Lin whispering, "Cases. Hah! Phony excuses. Men of the 1980s are all the same, Superintendent. They promise the world to get what they want and immediately forget you. I'm old-fashioned. I wish I had grown up in your era, when eligible men were principled gentlemen."

"We certainly were," Kiet lied, noticing some changes in the studio.

A camera was still arranged to televise a table and chair

183

backdropped by a white bedsheet; a technician was still working at a control panel. But there were two conspicuous additions to the scene.

A polished mahogany board was fastened vertically to the leading edge of the table, and fastened to the board was a plaque. Lettering on the plaque's circular border identified it as an official symbol or icon or some such of the Department of State of the United States of America.

At the sight of the buffed copper-and-teak coffin abutting the table, Kiet groaned. The man slumbering forever inside the box was a stocky, middle-aged Caucasian with graying, tightly curled hair. Kiet did not like to look at dead people and did so for just an instant, lest his stomach rebel. He did notice that the corpse's face was chalky white owing to the mortician's overuse of cosmetics. He thought it a miniature tragedy that Ambulance Al Selkirk would be dispatched to his Valhalla with his suntan obliterated.

"The eulogy by Ambassador Smithson I mentioned," Lin Aidit said. "The body was brought this evening and I've been commanded to have everything prepared before noon tomorrow."

"Splendid," Kiet said.

"When will you be ready to telecast?" Binh asked Lin.

Lin replied to Kiet, "We are ready now."

"Fantastic! Lin, do you have any makeup for the superintendent?"

"What is he talking about?" Lin asked Kiet.

"What are you talking about?" Kiet asked Binh.

"This," Binh said, holding the Golden Peacock.

"Oh my God, the rumors are true," Lin whispered.

"Forgive my evasions, Lin," Kiet said. "We had to keep the theft a secret."

"Makeup," Binh said to Lin.

"Makeup?" Kiet asked Binh.

"You have to apply makeup to remove facial glare," Binh

184

said. "No American anchorman would dream of going on camera without it."

"Anchorman?"

"You would be an ideal anchorman, Superintendent," Binh said. "You have charisma."

"So I have been informed."

"I have some rouge," Lin said.

"Do you see where I'm going with this?" Binh asked Kiet.

Kiet suddenly did. Though annoyed at himself for his narrow vision, his prejudice against technological progress, his resistance to change, he smiled and said, "Your brain typhoon is brilliant, Captain. We broadcast to Hickorn proof that the Golden Peacock is safe. Channel Seven is not only a refuge from Ridsa and the Vietnamese, it will be our tribunal."

Binh blushed happily and looked to Lin for approval. She was otherwise occupied, rummaging in her purse for rouge while conferring with the technician. She said, "Ninety seconds. We'll preempt 'Gunsmoke.'"

Binh slid the table and board aside and motioned Kiet to the chair. Kiet sat down and Binh placed the Golden Peacock on his thighs, saying, "Rivet on the camera, Superintendent. Eye contact is the key to credibility. I've seen anchormen go five minutes without blinking."

Kiet tried, unsuccessfully, imagining the long metal tube and its glass cyclops as a howitzer fired by hundreds of thousands of enraged Hickornians who had been wrenched from Dodge City without their permission. "Shouldn't we prepare a script I could read?"

"No time," Binh said as Lin dabbed perfumed powder on his face.

Kiet hoped that he didn't look as pretty as he smelled. "What shall I say?"

Binh fluffed Kiet's wispy hair with his comb and shrugged. "Wing it, Superintendent. I have faith. You'll be dynamite."

185

"Forty-five seconds," Lin said.

The Golden Peacock was cutting into Kiet's legs, numbing them. "No."

"Huh?" Binh said.

"Bring the table. I'll stand."

Binh reset the table, muttered, "The hell with them, no freebie plugs," then reversed it, jamming the U.S. State Department plaque against Kiet's toes. Lin spread ten fingers and tucked them, one by one.

Kiet rested the sacred headdress on the table and rose, watching Lin's digits vanish. He recollected yesterday's "Gunsmoke," Matt extinguishing the lynch mob, the necktie party. He had employed an exquisite balance of reason, compassion, and force. Yin and yang.

Kiet tucked his thumbs into his belt loops, assumed a wider stance, and said, "My Hickorn friends, good evening. You see before me our beloved Golden Peacock. This is irregular, but there is no reason to worry. It will be returned to the National Museum soon. I am interrupting your viewing to report the attempted theft of the Golden Peacock earlier in the evening. The courageous action of Dr. Latisa Chi, curator of the National Museum, foiled the robbery. He wrested the Golden Peacock from the criminals, who then escaped empty-handed. Dr. Chi could not identify the two robbers because of darkness, but he does know that one is male, the other female. They fled in a green Mercedes-Benz sedan. We are confident that they will be apprehended momentarily. Thank you for your kind indulgence. Good night."

Binh came forward and hugged Kiet. "Superintendent, you were magnificent!"

"Yup," Kiet said.

186

23

"'And how is yours, Bosha?"

Kiet and His Royal Highness, Prince Novisad Pakse, were at Luong Burgers, the day after Savhanakip, taking first bites from their cheeseburgers deluxe. Kiet measured Prince Pakse's expression before replying. His Royal Highness did not demand that the opinions of his subjects be in monotonous accord with his own, but Kiet felt it would be disrespectful to assert an opposite opinion on a question so trivial. Prince Pakse's expression was expressionless. Good; they were of a common mind.

"Edible," Kiet said.

"Edible," Prince Pakse said, nodding. "Blandly and inoffensively palatable."

Kiet lifted his bun and poured nic sau onto his perfectly circular meat patty, then spooned on sliced peppers. "I recommend these condiments, Your Highness."

Prince Pakse doctored his cheeseburger deluxe too, chewed and swallowed a mouthful, and said, "Flavor. It has flavor, Bosha. Again, your recommendation is flawless."

Kiet flushed with pleasure at the compliment, as he had

187

at Prince Pakse's use of his childhood nickname. No Luongan dictionary listed the word *bosha*. It had regional origins—Hickorn and southern Luong—and was a corruption of *bo shau*, a phrase literally defined as "stunted growth." In the vernacular, bosha meant runt. Kiet had not spurted in height until late adolescence, to the amusement of a few lifelong friends—His Royal Highness included—who had applied the nickname. As a boy Kiet had regarded it as teasingly cruel, but later in life he had come to accept Bosha as an affectionate diminutive.

"It has been a custom of ours to confer in the Royal Billiards Room at the conclusion of an important police case," Prince Pakse continued. "But I had never visited this—how do you say?—fast-food joint that so comforts the Western and Japanese tourists seated about us, whose hard currency we desire."

"And it is luncheon hour, Your Highness," Kiet said agreeably.

"I am happy that we could meet now, Bosha. I fly to Singapore early tomorrow for a billiards tournament. I have practice and official duties scheduled throughout the afternoon and the evening. The timing is good. Is this what the Westerners call a working lunch then, a power lunch?"

Prince Pakse was wearing a black tuxedo, the peculiar uniform of billiards tournaments. He also wore it during practice sessions to acclimate himself to a competition environment. Those who underestimated Luong's monarch derided him in such garb as an emaciated penguin. They did not repeat the insult to Prince Pakse's face, nor to Bamsan Kiet's. "Yes, Your Highness."

"You have solved countless crimes in your career, Bosha, but I do not remember a case as fraught with twists and turns as this one. Nor as heinous. To steal the Golden Peacock is unthinkable.

"I am not questioning your judgment—your handling of the case has been superb—but I wonder about the necessity of making Dr. Chi a hero. Did he not precipitate it all by conspiring with the late Mr. Selkirk?"

"Yes, he did, Your Highness. I was, uh, winging it."

"Winging it?"

"That is Captain Binh's Americanism for composing one's presentation as one speaks it. Minister Ridsa and Madame Mai were menaces at that time. The lie provided an indirect solution to the problem."

Prince Pakse nodded approvingly. "Your bulletin was received by the multitudes. The two scalawags barely escaped inside the Vietnamese embassy. That green Mercedes-Benz sedan you obligingly described was stoned and burned by a mob."

"Never again will I encourage vigilante law enforcement," Kiet said. "I promise."

Prince Pakse fluttered a bony hand. "You did what you had to do. Everyone praises you. They say you are a natural television performer. But I remain unclear as to Dr. Chi."

"I required a story that explained why I had the Peacock and not the criminals too. Chi might not be a plausible hero, but because he was at the National Museum on around-the-clock watch, he was the man thieves would most likely have encountered.

"The lie paid another dividend, Your Highness. Dr. Chi is tendering his retirement and has pledged to cooperate fully against Ridsa if Ridsa ever returns to Luong."

"You believe he's out of the country, Bosha?"

"I do, Your Highness. Ambassador Dang began packing that evening and it's my feeling that Ridsa was put on an airplane to Hanoi inside a crate with a diplomatic seal."

"To be notified by Dang the night before Savhanakip that he was being immediately recalled to Vietnam was a shock," Prince Pakse said. "With the information I have now, however, I would have expelled him just as quickly."

"He knew that, Your Highness."

"How the Vietnamese were able to insert themselves into

the scheme is beyond me," Prince Pakse said, shaking his head.

"We may never know everything, Your Highness, but it is doubtless a matter of business becoming politics. Chi and Selkirk and probably Chipperfield stole the Golden Peacock for profit. But then Chi made a bad mistake—by hiding the Golden Peacock in Ridsa's office, he invited Ridsa in as a player. Selkirk thought he could deal advantageously with the monster and that miscalculation cost him his life."

"Fop Tia?"

"The ultimate opportunist," Kiet said. "He was a former crony of Ridsa's and an Unknown Asia Tours investor. He knew everybody and guessed what was happening. Ex-Mayor Tia, by the way, flew to Bangkok this morning. I gave him the option of being formally arrested on an unspecified charge or signing a voluntary deportation order. He signed. If he ever again enters Luong, I'll jail him as an undesirable. We booked the seat next to him for Mr. Chipperfield. They will have a wealth of conversation topics, I'm sure."

"Tia thought he could renew his friendship with Ridsa and become his partner?"

"He thought wrong, Your Highness. Ridsa's ambition had outgrown him. Fop Tia had nothing to bargain."

Prince Pakse shook his head sadly. "What a horrible waste, Bosha. Ridsa was such a talented and industrious young man and I promoted him accordingly. He was our only ministry head not related to me by blood."

"I think that must have gnawed at him, Your Highness. He possibly felt that he could have ascended no higher."

"The continuance of nepotism is my greatest fault," Prince Pakse said. "I have learned a lesson. I am an old man. When I am gone, I want Luong to be ruled by good people. Henceforth, promotions will be decided less on family loyalty than merit. Perhaps, then, gifted youngsters with an interest in government will keep their ambitions on a constructive path.

"Bosha, you say that Tia had nothing to offer Ridsa. The Vietnamese obviously did. When did they become involved?"

"I don't know," Kiet said. "That element of the mess is the haziest. I would speculate that Ridsa developed a rapport with them soon after Luong and Vietnam established diplomatic relations. If any foreign power sweeps in and conquers us, logic dictates it to be Vietnam."

Prince Pakse smiled coldly. "Phorn Ridsa," he said. "Puppet dictator of the People's Republic of Luong."

"Indeed," Kiet said. "A Ridsa fantasy very easy to believe."

"When do you think they actually became involved in the Golden Peacock theft, Bosha?"

Bosha knew approximately. Twenty-four hours after Phorn Ridsa had crushed Ambulance Al Selkirk's skull with a stone Buddha, Madame Mai Le Trung was in Bamsan Kiet's bed. "Before Selkirk's body was cold, Your Highness."

"Those Vietnamese, they are as inclined to mischief as the Americans and Soviets," Prince Pakse said. "A new ambassador is scheduled to report within a month. I will greet him cheerfully. Our little kingdom cannot afford to antagonize Hanoi. But with your cooperation, Bosha, I will carefully monitor his activities."

"Absolutely," Kiet said.

"Ambassador Dang and the woman, the cultural attaché who was your soccer team liaison, left us at Savhanakip dawn. I was too busy readying for the celebration to bid them bon voyage. I dispatched the minister of agriculture and the minister of education to Hickorn International. Two vigorous, young ministers in lieu of a decrepit old prince, a substitution that should not cause the Vietnamese to lose face, don't you think?"

"Yes, Your Highness."

"They didn't appear to. They seemed to be embroiled in a squabble, uneasy at the presence of my emissaries. They would have much preferred to have been allowed to skulk off in privacy. My ministers said they behaved like husbands and wives do when there has been family dishonor and each holds the other to blame. They were chattering in Vietnamese, so we don't know what was said, but whenever Ambassador Dang raised his voice, he began coughing the frightful morning hack heavy cigarette smokers have. The woman in turn sneered and cut him with sharp words. If someone is to be held accountable at the Vietnamese Foreign Ministry, I would bet on poor, bloated little Dang. If they lock him in one of their political reeducation camps, it is what he deserves."

Kiet resumed eating his cheeseburger deluxe, an excuse not to reply.

Prince Pakse said, "That woman, her name is Mai?"

"Mai," Kiet mumbled, his mouth stuffed.

"You said previously that she provided your final clue."

Kiet swallowed. "Yes."

"Her tongue slipped and you knew she was pushing you toward a false assignment in Obon, just to get you out of Hickorn? She had been spying on you to learn what you knew and wanted to have you elsewhere when the Golden Peacock was found at the airport addressed to my dissipated idiot of a nephew in Paris?"

"Yes."

"If you had not recovered it at the Postal Office, Bosha, Ridsa and the Vietnamese might have had their way. My army and your police could not have kept order. I'd have been deposed, possibly killed. Hickorn would have been in flames. Our Indochinese brothers would have sent troops to restore peace in the region."

Kiet shrugged modestly.

"Dang introduced Mai to me at Savhanakip Penultimate,

192

Bosha. The woman is alluring, a visual treasure. If her bedroom skill parallels her beauty, she could enslave the best of men, don't you think?"

"Perhaps," Kiet said, eyes locked on his burger, his ears and neck on fire. "Nic sau is also tasty on the fried potatoes, Your Highness."

"I am sorry your adjutant, Captain Binh, could not dine with us."

"I tried to extend your invitation, but I couldn't locate him. It's his day off."

Prince Pakse smiled. "A day devoted to romance? I have heard stories about the lad."

"It is possible, Your Highness. He said he was going to attempt to mend fences. That seems a peculiar activity with which to win back friendship, but I didn't press for explanations. He has an appointment with Lin Aidit."

"Who is to be my next minister of tourism," Prince Pakse said, pounding his fist as if it were an official stamp. "Lin Aidit richly deserves to be the first beneficiary of my new promotion policy."

"Splendid, Your Highness!"

"I am sorry, too, Bosha, that Savhanakip police duties precluded you from attending the game."

Kiet groaned at the thought. He had missed the greatest moment in Luongan soccer history; Luong had tied Vietnam, 0–0. Knowledgeable spectators had reported that the Vietnamese forwards seemed listless, unable to organize in the Luongan zone. Luong's front-runners, on the other hand, were the equal of Vietnam's defenders. If not for several acrobatic saves by the Viet goalkeeper, Luong would have scored. Kiet wondered if the turmoil in the Vietnamese embassy had demoralized their side. One could only hope.

Prince Pakse continued. "Did you view Ambassador Smithson's eulogy?"

"No, Your Highness."

"Neither did I nor anybody else I know. Television is a wonderful advance for our kingdom, but who would be watching it during Savhanakip?"

Kiet smiled. "Nobody. Binh says that by preempting 'Gunsmoke' I, and I quote, 'waxed Smithson and Selkirk in the ratings.'"

"Bosha, you credit my other luncheon guest as being instrumental in the resolution of the case, and we've been ignoring him throughout our fascinating conversation." Prince Pakse turned to the man seated beside him. "I apologize for my discourtesy, sir. Are you enjoying your meal?"

Quoc, the leprous beggar with no nose, was midway through his third cheeseburger deluxe. He grinned and replied at length.

"What did he say, Bosha?"

"That it is a gastronomical masterpiece, Your Highness, a triad of extraordinary food assemblages. He is enjoying it."